Volunteer to Die

A Denise Reed Mystery

by

Mary E. Koppel

Copyright 2017 by Mary E. Koppel

For information, email **Cozy Cat Press**, cozycatpress@aol.com or visit our website at: www.cozycatpress.com

COZY CAT
PRESS

ISBN: 978-1-946063-21-2

Printed in the United States of America

Cover design by Paula Ellenberger
www.paulaellenberger.com

1 2 3 4 5 6 7 8 9 10

To my daughter, my family, my fabulous high school English teacher, and All Saints' Episcopal Church, Miami, Oklahoma. Thank you for your encouragement and support!

And thank you to Cindy Figueroa for the title of this book!

CHAPTER 1

"You need to get a job." I peered over the top of my laptop. Somehow, Mom had tip-toed into the kitchen in her clean white Keds and was now leaning against the refrigerator across from me. She sighed deeply and I knew I was in for the dreaded conversation.

I closed the cover of the laptop, not sure if Mom had seen that instead of sending resumés, I was actually reading the "Dear Prudence" column on *Slate*. Still, it was worth a shot: "Mom, I am looking…" Before I could say anything more, her perfectly manicured hand rose to stop my protests.

She cleared her throat and slipped into the chair next to me. "Denise, I know that you've been looking, even if you are reading some dreadful gossip website now, but what I mean is that you need to get out of the house. Don't worry about finding something perfect right now, just find a job." She smiled at me, with a kind of "you better do this or I might smother you in the night" grin.

I wanted to protest, but as usual, Mom was right, in her pearls, pressed blue cotton blouse and khaki slacks. She had worn some version of this uniform her whole existence. Even after retiring from real estate, she maintained this level of decorum as a matter of principle. My mother always said: "How you present yourself tells the world how it should treat you. It might not be right; but it's true." She believed it.

"Denise, you need to get out of the house." She reiterated her point. Her tone was concerned and mildly grossed out like I was emitting an odor. My mother perused my outfit. I could tell she wanted to reach out and pluck something off me.

I looked down at my orange sweat pants and purple college t-shirt complete with a coffee stain from earlier that morning. I still had crumbs in my lap from breakfast. My brown hair was pulled back in a greasy ponytail. I had not showered and I probably stank. I had not left the house much in a few days. For that matter, I hadn't really left the house in months—three months to be exact.

Of course, could you blame me? My mother's home was a renovated double shotgun house located on Joseph Street, in the Uptown neighborhood in New Orleans. A comfy wooden swing swung on the front porch, where one could sit and watch shoppers head to the Whole Foods on Magazine Street. This area of New Orleans was vibrant and lively with cute retail boutiques, a frightening amount of yoga studios and delicious cafes and restaurants. On Joseph Street, little houses, shotgun and double shotgun style from a bygone era, lined one side and huge new and expensive McMansions lined the other side of the street.

I would drop my daughter off at pre-school and then wander down to the coffeehouses on Magazine Street about once a day, ordering a café au lait. I might enter a shop or two, longing to purchase some bauble. Sometimes I'd even walk as far as Latter Library on St. Charles Avenue for the free Wi-Fi and to check out a few mysteries. But I hadn't really gone too far from mom's house because I was hiding out after losing my job. I felt embarrassed.

For the past three years I'd worked as a youth and family ministry coordinator at a large church in New Orleans. Sure, that might sound kind of impressive, but actually my work entailed calling people and persuading them to participate in church events, eating pizza with teenagers, and rolling my eyes at the senior pastor when he wasn't looking. I enjoyed what I did, but I thought I wanted something different.

I had two degrees. I was heading into my late thirties and divorced. Only a few years before, I'd adopted my daughter. With her arrival, my priorities had shifted. Somehow, playing hide and go seek with 5th graders felt limiting. I knew that I could do more.

Not to go in to a lot of details, but I'd managed to talk myself out of my own job one afternoon when talking to the lead pastor about my desire to explore more in my ministry. I remember him smiling and asking if perhaps I'd be happier somewhere else. At the time, I didn't pick up on what he was putting down, so I nodded yes. Finances were getting tight at the church, and I walked right into my own budget cut. I left the position with a lot of bravado, thinking that I'd be walking into a new position fairly quickly. This would be an opportunity for me. Of course, in ministry, there are not a ton of full time positions.

So, I was an over-educated youth minister who was out on my butt. More specifically, I was an over-educated 34-year-old, divorced, single mother youth minister who was gaining weight steadily and living with her mother for the last three months. Strange things start to happen when you stop working for a few months. One is that you do not start that novel that you always said you would start writing if you had time because you are totally freaking out about becoming broke and homeless. The other is that you start questioning every decision you ever made and you wonder if your judgment might only be suited to judge a hotdog eating competition. At the moment, between sending out resumés and receiving constant rejections, I fluctuated between freaking out and feeling like a fool. Yep, that sums it up.

"Denise, you need to kick yourself in the butt and get out there! Now, get dressed." She stopped for emphasis. "You definitely should take a shower first." I bristled at her comment, but inwardly I agreed. "Also, make sure that what you wear is something appropriate." She said that with a knowing nod. I wanted to roll my eyes. As if I was going to wear a mid-drift bearing top and daisy dukes? "You're coming with me this morning," I heard her say as she walked to her bedroom. I guess we were going somewhere. Oh, goody!

CHAPTER 2

Mom pressed the bell and the gate cranked open. We pulled into the parking lot of Riverview. "What are we doing here?" What were we doing there? Riverview was the most exclusive senior living/nursing home in the city. I had been there a few times, visiting a great aunt who had long since died. The facility was lovely. It was located where Broadway meets the Mississippi River's levy, only a few blocks from Audubon Park and Zoo, in Uptown New Orleans. Seven floors rose high above the oak-lined avenue, offering beautiful views of the levies and Mississippi River on one side and Audubon Park on the other. The building's tag line was something like: "Living with a river view." I wonder how many consultants it took to come up with that gem. I suppose I could smirk, but those consultants were getting paid.

I followed mom into the building and she took off at a clip. We wandered through the tasteful oak-paneled lobby with its marble floors, to the mirrored elevators. She pressed the button for the second floor. "Mom?" I think she was ignoring me. She was quiet and thoughtful on the quick ride up.

"I hope we aren't late," she muttered. She still hadn't answered my original question. I asked again: "What are we doing here, Mother?"

My mother looked at me with mild annoyance. She inspected my outfit, purple sweater with black slacks. I couldn't believe how tight the pants felt. I actually hadn't snapped the top button for fear it would pop off and hit someone in the head. Clearly, she could tell the pants were a shade too tight. I instinctively sucked in as she reached over and removed invisible lint from my sweater.

The elevator doors opened and I followed her again, this time down a pastel-carpeted hallway to an activity room. All the chairs were arranged to face a table with a little cross and candles on it. Finally, Mom turned and looked at me: "I volunteer here for the Tuesday service, each congregation takes a turn." With that, she ran to the front table and checked in with the minister. I recognized the man in the collar at the front as one of my old work colleagues. He waved while I waved and turned a little red. This was going to be uncomfortable.

I looked around the room. I needed to find a way to avoid speaking with my old workmate. Tables covered with half-done puzzles or crafts lined the walls, I walked over and looked down at an almost completed Eiffel Tower, not sure what to do with myself. I could see in my peripheral vision that Rev. Todd was about to walk over to me. Thankfully, the room slowly filled with residents escorted by the staff. Some entered with walkers and some entered in wheelchairs. I found a seat in the back.

The service began and I zoned out during the familiar words until I felt a tug on my sleeve. "I forgot my sweater, Tina; you need to go get my sweater." I looked at the frail woman beside me. "Did you hear me, Tina?" She raised her voice just shy of a shout which was followed by a roomful of "shhh."

"Ma'am, I'm not Tina," I whispered. I wanted to scoot my chair away from her, but I was penned in by a sleeping gentleman in a wheelchair on the other side of me.

"What? Why won't you go get my sweater?" I looked around the room for an aide. Apparently, everyone was on a smoke break. A couple of people in scrubs with small lavender ribbons pinned to them leaned against the back wall. They ignored the outburst. One looked at a cellphone and the other avoided looking in this woman's direction. Another round of "shhs" was accompanied with indignant stares. I whispered a little louder this time: "My name is Denise; I'm not Tina. I don't know where your sweater is."

The woman was undeterred: "Just take me back to get my sweater, Tina!" At this point, I could feel my mother's stare from the front of the room. Through smiling clenched teeth, I heard her say: "Yes, Tina, why don't you take her to get her sweater?" Okay.

I stood up and offered the woman my arm as she noisily rose from her seat. We were only about three chairs from the room's entrance, but moving through walkers proved to be perilous. I caught the woman's arm twice as she stumbled.

At last, we made our way to the hallway. I looked down the hallway, left and right. Everything looked the same, pastel carpet, non-descript wood paneling and watercolor prints for artwork with brass numbered grey doorways. "So, where is your room?" I asked.

"It's around here somewhere. I can't quite remember right now. Let's walk around until something looks familiar." The woman looked up at me and smiled. I sighed as we began our stroll. I guess this beat sitting around in sweatpants. It certainly beat listening to one of Rev. Todd's sermons.

Perhaps if we started walking, we would arrive at a nursing station and someone would know where this little lady belonged, and who Tina was, and where my friend could find her sweater. We wandered down the hallway that was more reminiscent of a Hampton Inn than a nursing facility. After walking past a dozen more non-descript rooms, we came upon a lounge with plush chairs, faux silk-covered sofas and the television blaring. Two gentlemen sat in front of the screen, maybe a little too close. One was snoring and the other seemed to be engrossed in the soap opera on the screen.

"Let's stop here; I need a rest." The lady immediately sank into an overstuffed pink loveseat. I thought perhaps this was my escape, but she patted the seat next to her. I sat down and she immediately took my hand tightly in her own.

"I have a confession to make. I know you're not Tina and I don't need my sweater." She dug into her large purse and produced a cream-colored cardigan. "What's your name again?" At this point, the woman locked her stare on me. I looked back into somewhat milky blue eyes.

"My name is Denise Reed." I laughed a little to myself. I guess I wasn't the only one trying to sneak out of a church service early.

"My name is Louise Butler," she said. "You can call me Ms. Butler, for now." She smiled like she might smile at a small child. I nodded. Her statement was strange, because I didn't plan on staying around long. She turned her head to the side and examined me carefully.

"Denise, you look very familiar. You look a lot like one of my former students, but I'm sure you're too young. What's your mother's name?" She listened intently to my answer.

"Her name is Margaret Reed, but her maiden name was Cline. She helps with the service on Tuesdays." When I spoke my mother's maiden name, Ms. Butler leaned back and shook her head vigorously. I thought it was strange that she thought I looked like my mother. Often people said I looked like my father. My mother was petite and lean and I was, well, curvy and tall.

"Yes, that's right! I can see it around your eyes, very inquisitive eyes. She was an excellent student. One of the smartest in her class! I thought that might have been her, but I usually sit in the back and cannot see that well. I always read about her doing something in the paper. What a small world." Ms. Butler reflected for a moment. I smiled and edged toward standing up and moving away.

"Denise, you seem like a nice girl too, going to church and all, with your mother. Not like a lot of other ones around here. Some of them could use a little church, if you know what I mean." She looked around as if she thought an orderly or aide would walk past right at that moment.

"Oh, I'm sure they aren't all bad. Surely Tina is nice," I tried to reassure. "Well, I better get back to church." I moved to get up, but Ms. Butler took hold of my hand again and tightened her grip.

"Yes, Tina was nice, and that's what got her killed." That stopped me right in my tracks.

"Excuse me; what did you say?" I wasn't sure what the woman had said. Surely I misunderstood or she was nuttier than a fruitcake.

"They killed her. At least, I think they did. They got rid of her because she was asking too many questions." I looked at her face, trying to gauge if she just had an addled mind.

"Are you sure she didn't just quit? Maybe she got fired? Lots of people get fired all the time," I suggested as she shook her head vigorously.

Ms. Butler began to cry quietly. Perhaps this was just a sign of dementia or a terrible misunderstanding where a little old lady missed an orderly. Either way, I suppose that I could humor her. I had nowhere else to be. I sat down next to her and dug through my purse until I found a stack of McDonald's napkins. I handed her one.

"What makes you think that someone killed Tina?" Ms. Butler dabbed her tears. She stopped abruptly and looked closely at me again. I think this time she was wondering whether or not I thought she was crazy. I might have, but I was at least going to look like I was taking her concern seriously. She was elderly, for crying out loud.

"Two weeks ago, my friend Mrs. Lees went on hospice. She had a terrible bout with cancer, but frankly it didn't bother her too much. Doris never complained; German stock, you know." She shook her head knowingly. "Except about hemorrhoids; she would complain about those. Heck, we all complain about those. They are terrible. But like I said, she never really complained in a complainy kind of way."

I was wondering what differentiated a "complainy-kind of way" of complaining versus the usual complaining, but this story was getting long. "Ms. Butler, what does this have to do with Tina?" Ms. Butler shook her head, as if shaking out the cobwebs.

"Of course, the point. The point is that Doris also had a beautiful Wedgewood heart necklace that she wore. I always admired it, and I guess Doris realized that, so she said that when she died I could have it." I wasn't sure just where this was going and obviously that showed on my face, so she continued: "Well, Mrs. Lees died in the evening. They made an announcement during dinner, so I asked Tina to check about my, I mean, Doris' necklace, because Tina would probably be with the group that would clean up Doris before her family came. I wanted her to ask the family about it when they came. Well, when Doris' daughter came, Tina asked about the necklace. The two looked for it, but it was nowhere to be found." Ms. Butler *tsk*ed and frowned.

"Uh-huh." I refrained from making the "wrap it up motion with my hands," but I still wondered where a missing necklace led to a dead orderly.

"Tina was very conscientious. I'm sure that she reported the theft to that miserable sow Cramer, the head administrator, and to Dr. Martin. Cramer and her band of thieves must have murdered Tina for revealing their crime." At this point she let out a proud puff. Something told me that Ms. Butler might have watched one episode too many of *Murder She Wrote* in the 80s.

"Ms. Butler, do you watch a lot of mystery shows? Anything could have happened to that necklace after your friend died. Her daughter could have just taken it and didn't want to give it to you. It could be lost somewhere in that room. It wasn't necessarily theft." At this point, I could see the disappointment on her face. The two gentlemen who I'd thought were either watching television too closely or sleeping moved right next to me. They both loomed over me.

"Miss Louise ain't making this up. Toots here had his purple heart stolen, and they also stole $200 from under Roger's mattress. Cramer says maybe they'd misplaced them. She wouldn't lift a finger." The old man snorted and his friend "Toots" (I shuddered to think how he got his nickname) laughed mirthlessly. He stared down at me from a hunched over position, shaking his finger. Surprisingly, the boney finger in my face was a little menacing for someone I suspected could fall over and break a hip just by chewing gum too vigorously. I rearranged myself to avoid an accidental poke in the eye.

"That's enough, Nolan." Ms. Butler pushed his hand from my face. He dropped his hand by his side and he mumbled "sorry."

"Okay, I'm sure there probably is someone stealing here," I said to the little group. "I'm sure that if you took this complaint to the administration here, they would investigate and fire that person and probably press charges, but none of this necessarily means that Tina was murdered. How do you know she was murdered?"

"We haven't seen her since she spoke to Cramer and Dr. Martin. They're trying to protect their reputation at any cost." The man spoke the last sentence low. I looked at the three. They got quiet, as a pimply faced orderly with headphones wandered down the hall with his cleaning supplies.

"Are you sure she wasn't just fired?"

"Of course they fired her!" the three answered in a loud chorus and looked at me incredulously.

"So, how do you know that she isn't at home?" Toots threw his hands up and mumbled to himself. I thought I heard him say "idiot," but I couldn't be sure. The other man stomped his foot. At this point, Ms. Butler reached into her purse and pulled out the newspaper.

Ms. Butler handed the folded paper to me: "Because I read the obituaries every morning."

CHAPTER 3

Before I could finish reading the obituary for Christina "Tina" Moore, the three scattered from me. A nurse's aide walked down the corridor. Toots and his friend returned to their *too close* television watching/snoring. Ms. Butler moved quickly down the hallway in the opposite direction from the aide.

As the aide got closer, I noticed that his uniform clung to his muscles. The guy looked like Jason Stratham in scrubs. Something told me that he probably had a lot of old and young lady admirers at Riverview. Once Ms. Butler passed the aide, she stopped briefly and admired the man's rear with a smile of approval. He looked directly at me and smiled slowly. I just stared like an idiot.

I looked back down at the newspaper in my lap. I read the obituary of the 24-year-old mother of two— Brandon and Bryce—also survived by her brother Antony and mother Claudette Moore. It said she was in an accident. The obituary only had about five lines. Her visitation and funeral were at Thomas and Family Funeral Home in Metairie.

Could this tale be true? I shook my head and stood up. Who cared if it was true? It was none of my business. I should really get back to that activity room, but I was lost. How far had I walked from the room and how often had I turned? Everything looked the same.

I decided to head to the exit. If I found an exit, I'd probably find an elevator. I decided that I'd meet my mother in the lobby. Surely, the church service was over by now, so I headed toward the closest elevator.

When I found the elevator, I rode to the first floor. I immediately looked for a garbage can to throw away the newspaper. I tossed the paper in a can next to the front desk, and sat on the bench opposite the elevators. I tried pushing the story and obituary from my mind, but I kept returning to the "mother of two" part. How terrible to leave behind her babies? Did someone really kill her because she reported a theft?

I stood up and slowly paced the room. What in the world was taking my mother so long? Why was I still thinking about this woman? My eye caught the nameplate on the office door behind the front desk: Cramer. I was about to approach the desk and ask to speak to her when the elevator door dinged and my mother emerged. I guess that settled it. I would head home, slip on my orange sweat pants, and forget Tina Moore.

"Where did you run off to?" my mother asked. "Father Todd wanted a chance to speak with you, but you disappeared with that little woman. Did she find her sweater?" She rearranged her purse on her shoulder and turned towards me as we walked out the building.

"Mom, I don't want to talk with Father Todd." I groaned inwardly, imagining how uncomfortable that conversation would have been. Half the time we'd spent together at St. Christopher's was complaining about our boss, but where I would voice my concerns to the boss, at times, he always remained silent. His excuse was "you have to ask yourself if you can work for someone you don't respect." He never offered his answer, but he still worked at St. Christopher's. I guess that my answer to that question was no. I suppose that I could take comfort in that I actually had made a change, a stupid, stupid change.

"I know that you feel sheepish about anything having to do with St. Christopher's, but wasn't he a friend?" she reminded me with tenderness. She gave me a playful pinch. I could probably have used a few friends right now. Actually, I could have used a job right then. Maybe he was on to something, working for someone you don't respect.

I went on and answered my mom's original question, omitting any mention of thieves or murder. "We found her sweater. Turns out that she knows you. Do you remember Ms. Butler?"

My mother stopped abruptly. "That was Louise Butler?" Her eyes squinted and her lips pursed, "Her class was the only class in which I received a B plus." She enunciated every word like she was about to snarl. My mother frowned momentarily and then she continued her trek to the car.

"B plus isn't a bad grade," I said to my mother. She certainly had told me that when I was in high school.

"I made all *A*'s." Of course she did. We entered the car in silence.

As I buckled my seatbelt, I asked, "Did you hear about that aide, Tina Moore?" My mother was still silent. She checked her face in the visor, pushing an invisible stray hair behind her ear.

"Yes, that was terrible. Young woman and very sweet." She shook her head, snapping on her belt and starting the car. "Why are you bringing that up? Did someone mention her?"

"Yes, Ms. Butler mentioned her." I thought about saying something about the old woman's suspicions, but I kept quiet.

"I'm sure she probably would. I imagine a lot of the residents would. They're like a family at Riverview." With that, my mom put on the radio and we rode home. We rolled down Leake Avenue as it turned into

Magazine Street. Even at midday on a Tuesday, I could see people jogging through Audubon Park.

When we arrived at the house, my mother stopped the car. She grabbed my forearm before I could exit the vehicle. "You really need to find something to do, Denise."

CHAPTER 4

That afternoon, I decided against hunkering down at home after my mother's warning and I discovered that my orange sweatpants had a hole in the crotch. I took the sign and I headed to Latter Library with my laptop, determined to send out more resumés. Instead, I climbed the elegant curving staircase to the fiction section and made my way to the mysteries. I read the back of about a dozen books when my phone dinged with a message. I looked down and saw a text from my old boss: "Driving past Latter Library; can see your car. Are you available this afternoon at 4:30?" The phone dinged again with another text. This time it was a praying hands emoji.

I groaned inwardly. This is why you don't put an Episcopal shield on the back of your car. I wondered what he might want, but I dreaded talking to the man. He made me feel like a moron. I could have ignored the text, but I knew another and then another text was coming, possibly followed by a call if there was something he wanted. I needed to respond and shut him down.

I wracked my brain with a good excuse for not talking to the man. After all, should anyone ever have to talk to their old boss again, especially after he'd pushed you right out the door? I wrote and erased about a dozen responses and was about to tell him where to shove his message when I remembered the paper and typed out: "Going to a visitation at 4; sorry."

I ran down the stairs, without a book and left the building. I immediately headed to my car and started the engine. I saw his vehicle pull into the entrance of the parking lot as I sped out the exit. For a moment, we exchanged glances as I sped away. Where could I go now?

I couldn't go home yet. I was driving my mother crazy. It was still too early to pick up Emily. I didn't want a coffee. Maybe I would go to that visitation. Before I realized it, I was pulling into the parking lot of Thomas and Family on Causeway Boulevard in Metairie.

Thomas and Family was a beige brick building, surrounded by immaculate landscaping and shaded by several large crepe myrtles. Once inside, I saw that there were three parlors in this particular funeral home, also all in various shades of beige. They could not be more plain, but for the flowers. Tina Moore's visitation was in one of the smaller rooms. The first thing I noticed was the scent of carnations and lilies. The room was packed with white and purple flowers, but little more.

I saw who I assumed was Tina's mother looking into the casket. She was completely still and silent. Sitting in chairs, near the opened casket were curly brown-haired twin boys in black suits with purple bow ties. I judged them to be about my Emily's age. They wiggled and giggled softly. No one else was in the room. I thought that perhaps this was a bad idea and went to walk away, when she addressed me, without turning around: "Hello?"

"Uh, yes, hello, you must be Mrs. Moore. I was coming to pay my respects. I am so sorry for your loss." I moved toward her with my hand outstretched. She immediately turned towards me and threw herself into my arms. She began to bark out tears. With her tears, the two boys froze and then they too began to wail.

"Oh God, why my baby?" Mrs. Moore sobbed on my shoulder. I could feel the wetness through my shirt. I held her and said nothing. I knew that there was nothing that I could say. Eventually, she sighed heavily and looked at me. Two sets of little arms wrapped around my thighs and held on.

I looked down into their beautiful brown eyes, and their little doe eyes looked up at me, as if looking for reassurance. I smiled at the boys, reached down and patted them both on their backs. I could feel my heart breaking.

Mrs. Moore shooed the boys and pointed to the chairs. They ran to their seats and sat, dutifully returning to their squirming and giggling. I watched them for a little bit while they settled back on their perches.

She stepped back from me and wiped her nose with the back of her hand and then wiped her hand on her black dress. She sighed again and looked at me: "How did you know my Tina?" I examined the woman more closely.

She was a fairly young woman, maybe in her fifties. She could not be that much older than me. Her skin was smooth, and grey only touched the very edges of her brown curly hair.

"Riverview," was all I could squeak out. She nodded at me.

"She loved working there. She loved people. I was so angry when they fired her for nothing, but she kept saying: 'It'll be okay, Mom,' when we were on the phone. It wasn't okay. Firing someone for telling the truth! Tina never took a thing in her life and she's the one who gets fired?" She hiccupped and looked at me for a response. I didn't speak, not sure what even to say and not wanting to say too much or the wrong thing.

"That's terrible," was all I could answer. Mrs. Moore turned towards one of the flower arrangements. She touched the petals of one of the flowers. The arrangement was magnificent, the largest one in the room actually. Unlike the other, smaller arrangements, this one had lavender orchids and enormous white roses. Ms. Moore leaned down and sniffed a white rose.

"Tina loved the smell of roses. This is nice. Thank you." She smiled and looked at me as if I had given the flowers. I smiled back and glanced at the envelope tucked into the stand. I saw the unmistakable Riverview logo.

"Would you like to see her?" Mrs. Moore asked earnestly. I wanted to shout: "Hell no!" Instead, I nodded my head and she gestured to the casket. I looked down at what was once Tina Moore. I blanched when I saw her. The similarities were shocking. She could have been my younger sister. Certainly she was petite, but her face was oval like mine, and her hair was almost the same style and color as my own.

She wore a lavender silk blouse and a gold cross. Her garish make-up could barely cover what must have been terrible bruising to her face. Mrs. Moore reached down and caressed her daughter's cold cheek, "They did a nice job." I answered with a simple "yes," despite the discomfort I felt.

Finally, some other people entered the room and Mrs. Moore wandered towards them as I wandered out. On my way out the door, I saw the aide from earlier in the day. This time he had a black sweatshirt over his scrubs. I nodded at him and headed for my car.

In the parking lot, there was now a van from Riverview and a few residents were climbing out. I saw Mrs. Butler climb down. I attempted to make my way to my car without making eye contact, but somehow the woman saw me through her coke bottle glasses. She waved me over. I sighed and walked to her.

"You went by?" Ms. Butler asked. I shook my head yes. "Why?"

"It seemed like the right thing to do, I guess," I answered, still feeling the little arms wrapped around my thighs.

"It was the right thing to do. Even if we don't know people, we need to honor life. People deserve to be remembered." She spoke so solemnly. I knew she was not just speaking about Tina Moore's death. "How was her mother taking it?"

"I don't know. She was sad. This is so sad." I prayed that Mrs. Moore had support. From all the flowers I saw, many people must have cared for Tina. Would they be there for her mother and her sons? I hoped so.

She scanned the building and her gaze fell on something or someone. She reflected a while and then spoke again. "You're a kind girl, Denise, I can tell. Would you come by and see me again at Riverview? Maybe next Tuesday?"

I wasn't sure how I would answer. The driver who'd accompanied the group of seniors was motioning for them to enter the funeral home. She reached out and took my hand, demanding my reply. What would it hurt to humor the woman? It wasn't like I was working right now.

"Okay. I'll see you when I come next week." I gave her hand a squeeze and let go. I guess my social calendar was beginning to fill up.

CHAPTER 5

The next week, I accompanied my mother to Riverview for the service. I could tell she was shocked that I would come again, but I also think she felt good, like somehow she'd accomplished helping her daughter find some meaning in her unemployed life. Little did she know I just wanted to see how Ms. Butler was doing.

In the activity room, I waited for Ms. Butler to arrive. The room filled, but I didn't see my new friend yet. When I'd finally resigned myself to sitting through the little service, I heard a "psst" from the back of the room. Somehow I knew it had to be her. When I turned around, she was waving at me from the doorway.

I made my way to her quickly. In the hallway, she waved me down the hall. I was surprised at how quickly she could move, but I followed. We stood in front of a doorway and she unlocked the door. Without a word, she signaled for me to enter, so I followed her in.

"Please sit down, Denise." I sat on a chintz love seat that faced two matching chairs. The room looked like a page out of *Southern Living* magazine, but the most beautiful part was the window that looked at the levy. The Riverview motto was not lying. I could see the top of some huge ship making its way down the Mississippi.

Ms. Butler sat in one of the chairs and looked at me sweetly: "Thank you so much for coming back. I wasn't sure you would." I smiled at her. She smiled back and then her face dropped, "Oh, my goodness, my manners. Would you like some sherry?" She stood up and walked over to the little kitchen near the door. Before I could answer, she returned with a silver tray with a crystal decanter filled with red liquid and two small crystal glasses. She began to pour and handed me a glass: "Tell me about yourself, Denise."

CHAPTER 6

After two glasses of disgusting liquid, Louise and I were on a first name basis. I was surprised how much I enjoyed talking to her and how interesting she was. I told her about my life, my daughter, my job and losing my job. I was at loose ends, but she just listened.

Louise told me her story. She grew up in New Orleans and attended Newcomb, majoring in art, much to her family's chagrin. She ran off to Paris with a buddy, and lived abroad for ten years, teaching English, after she finished an MFA at Barnard and stayed two extra years in New York, marrying a musician 20 years her senior who turned out to be gay but a fabulous best friend. Mr. Butler abruptly died of a heart attack at 55. So, she returned to New Orleans and taught English and Art History at a small girl's school for the next 35 years, loving every minute of it.

We both laughed. "I guess we needed to meet each other, Denise." Louise smiled at me, and then she looked down at her watch, "Oh my, you better get back to the service or you'll miss your ride."

I sat there a moment, a little sad. I guess I didn't realize how much I needed to tell my story to someone other than my mother. "Thank you, Ms. Butler."

"Louise," she corrected. We were both quiet for a while.

"Louise, why did you talk to me last week?" I thought about our original encounter. Last Tuesday had certainly gone a direction than I'd expected.

"When I was sitting next to you at the service, I might have fallen asleep," she admitted. "When I woke up, I looked at you quickly and thought you were Tina. I thought that Tina was back and then I realized you weren't her. She was much shorter and her hair was a little lighter." She stopped talking. We sat in silence until she continued, "I felt sad and angry. I wanted to get out of there before I got emotional. Thank you for helping me on Tuesday."

"You really liked Tina Moore," I stated and she just smiled.

"I know that it sounds cliché: a sweet young woman shows kindness to an old lady, but you really should have met her. She was always cheerful and kind. She would stop whatever she was doing and speak with you. On her breaks, she would sometimes come over and visit me or some of the other residents. Certainly I get around better than most my age, but I don't get a lot of visitors." She looked at me. I felt such warmth from her words, but I also felt a pang of sorrow. She was lonely.

"Do you really think someone here at Riverview could have murdered Tina Moore? The obituary said she was hit by a car. That sounds like a terrible accident, not a murder." Louise thought for a moment. She reached towards the tray and poured another sherry.

"I hear you, Denise. I don't know who did this to her, but I feel it in my bones that it wasn't just an accident. All I know is that she reported that necklace missing, was gone at the end of the day, and then she was dead." She offered to fill my glass, but I placed my hand over the rim.

"If you really think so, maybe you should talk to the police about your suspicion." I waited for her response. She looked down a moment, biting her lip.

"Denise, I'm not sure if you noticed, but I'm an old woman living in a fancy nursing home." We both laughed a little as she continued, "Old people often 'misplace' things or 'imagine' things. They just think that I'm a batty old lady."

"You went to the police?" I was surprised. She shook her head.

"I spoke to an officer. I told him what I told you about the necklace and the thefts and my suspicions, but they just patted my hand and told me that Tina's death was a terrible accident and asked if I had any proof about the thefts. I had no proof." She stopped abruptly and thought for a moment. She repeated slowly: "I have no proof."

She stood up and walked to her window and looked out at the levy. Louise swung around and looked at me: "I just need to find proof." I did not like where this was going.

"Louise, what are you saying?" I shifted in my seat, leaning closer. I had a feeling that my new friend might be contemplating something dangerous. She looked at me and smiled.

"You better get going, Denise." With that, she dismissed me. We walked towards her door and she hugged me. "I hope that you'll come back and see me." I smiled at her, but in the back of my head a worry gnawed at me.

CHAPTER 7

I started visiting Louise each week on Tuesday over the next three weeks. We arranged that I would wait in the activity room until she came and then we would sneak out the back of the service. At her suite, every time, she offered and poured the dreadful sherry, as we talked about our families and lives. I told her about books I was reading. She told me Riverview gossip.

"How goes your job search?" Louise poured the sherry to the very rim of my glass. I carefully brought it to my lips and sipped. I just shrugged. What could I say? I felt like each time I'd come close to a new position, something would happen. I'd mess up the interview. The job would go to someone else. It felt like I was never what anyone was looking for. Thinking about my job search, I began to get a little tearful.

"Denise, I know losing your job was a blow to your confidence. You're giving your old job and old boss too much power over you. Don't let whether you have a position or not dictate how much you're worth. You're a good person. You're here, visiting with an old lady. Who else would do that willingly without being paid? Why do you come and see me?" she asked. I thought about it. Why was I there again?

"Maybe my motives are not so pure. Maybe I'm using spending a little time with you to avoid my problems and other people. Maybe I don't have anything else to do," I answered honestly. I felt a little bad about my admission. She just smiled at me.

"Do you really believe that? You think that you don't have anything else to do?" she asked incredulously. I wasn't sure what she meant. I stared at my lap. The tears started to roll.

"I don't know what to do. I feel like I can't do anything." I mumbled my answer. Louise moved right next to me.

"Look at me, Denise. You do plenty. You *can* do plenty! You have a lot more resources and skills than you give yourself credit for. Right now you might not be able to see it, but I do. You take care of your daughter. From what you've told me and what I've heard about St. Christopher's, you did a good job in your former position. Remember, you left *them*. They did not kick you out. You are kind and curious, probably the best qualities any person could have. You're going to be just fine." She spoke with conviction. She patted me on my shoulder and stood up and returned to her chair.

"How do you know?" I sniffed. I realized that I felt frightened about the future. How would I take care of my daughter if I didn't find a job?

"Because I'm old and wise. You'll be fine," she proclaimed and then chuckled. I wiped my tears with the back of my hand. She reached a tissue from the side table and handed it to me. "Does talking with me help you?" I nodded my head. I did feel better. I might be unsure at the moment of what would happen next in my life, but it felt good to be reminded that I was not without hope. She continued, "What is it that Martha Stewart always says? It's a good thing?" We both laughed. For the first time in three months, I felt lighter.

"Okay then, Denise, it's settled! Now I have a question for you. I need your help."

"What do you need, Louise?" I thought that I knew where this conversation was going. Perhaps she would recommend therapy to me or that I should take up a new hobby. Maybe jogging? I hoped it wasn't jogging.

"I need your help to find proof that someone is stealing here at Riverview and that someone killed Tina Moore." I was struck dumb. She definitely was not recommending jogging. Louise could not have been clearer and yet, somehow, I was in a fog. When had a sweet, meaningful conversation about the uncertainty of life turned to an episode of *Matlock*?

"You cannot be serious." I tried to laugh, but it caught in my throat. Louise leaned toward me, her gaze filled with the intensity of a laser beam.

"Denise, I've thought about this," she replied through clenched teeth. Her resolve was steel.

"I don't know the first thing about investigating a crime. I don't even know where to start. Besides, I'm only here once a week, if that." After her suggestion, I might drop my visits to never.

"Of course you know how to investigate; you read books, don't you? You're resourceful and curious. I can tell that people like talking to you. I can help you too. I watch a lot of police procedurals. I'm just looking for enough proof to take to the police," Louise pleaded with me. She pressed her palms together.

"I cannot do this." I shook my head. Louise leaned back in her chair and pursed her lips.

"Then I will investigate myself!" she shot back. My mouth gaped open. She continued: "That's right; a feeble old woman will investigate thieving murderers. I'm sure that I can handle it." Guilt. She was using guilt with a master's level of expertise.

I slumped into the couch and folded my arms. "Okay, Louise; I'll help you. What do you propose that I do?"

CHAPTER 8

I stood at the Riverview reception desk waiting for the receptionist to look up from her phone conversation. She smiled and lifted one finger. I pulled on the bottom of my grey jacket. It had been awhile since I'd worn this suit. I was surprised that I could still button it, but to be safe, I'd put on my tightest Spanx possible. I was barely breathing. I looked at the beautiful oak desk. I wondered how often someone had to wipe off fingerprints.

As if I was thinking out loud, an orderly began to spray the desk with furniture polish and wipe. The young man bobbed his head, listening to his music and wiped across the desk. He moved right next to me, a little too close, and mumbled, "excuse me."

I stepped back and he continued across the desk. At last, the young receptionist ended her conversation and looked at me expectantly. I asked if I might see Ms. Cramer.

I could feel sweat under my arms. My heart raced. Why had I agreed to attempt this?

Almost before I could say her name, the oak door behind the receptionist swung open. The creature that emerged looked like a real life version of Aunt Selma from *The Simpsons* stuffed into a blue pinstriped pant suit with a ruffled red blouse. She smiled warmly at me, but somehow I just didn't believe it.

"Hello, I'm Ms. Cramer of Riverview, how may I help you?"

I stuttered for a moment and then the words and story I'd rehearsed with Louise kicked in: "I'm looking for a job." I carefully lifted my resumé, my hand shaking. Ms. Cramer took the sheet from my hand and scanned it. She leaned over the reception desk and whispered something to the receptionist.

She looked again at the resumé in her hand. I had fully expected Ms. Cramer to politely and quickly blow me off. I would humor Louise, knowing full well that there was no way I'd get a job at Riverview, especially just by showing up unannounced. I would check out Ms. Cramer to see if the woman might be someone who would steal from the elderly or murder a young mother. I waited for her smile to drop, but instead, she invited me into her office and offered me a seat.

The office felt like a large closet with a huge metal desk, filing cabinets, and two folding chairs for visitors. Everything that visitors saw at Riverview looked so elegant and clean, but I guess that most people didn't enter the office. I wondered what else was a façade at Riverview.

Ms. Cramer looked expectantly at me. I realized that I was out of my depth. At this moment, I couldn't tell anything about this woman, except that she might have an outrageous fashion sense given that red blouse. I smiled at her and decided my best bet was to tell the truth, omitting my conversations with Ms. Butler.

"I know I just blurted that out earlier. I was here this morning with my mother, assisting with the church service. I've been coming for a couple of weeks. So, I realized, well, I wondered what it might take to get a job here—or a place like here."

"There is no other place *like* Riverview." She emphasized the "like." Clearly, it was a point of pride with her. I nodded in agreement with Ms. Cramer. She focused on me the way a cat looks at you, which is to say, completely and inscrutably. I had no idea why this woman had not just blown me off.

Wait, I knew what her technique was. She was going to let me talk and talk until I wore myself out or had enough rope to hang myself. I had used the same method myself when listening to church members' problems or complaints at my old position. I realized now that I was getting close to that length.

"Yes, Riverview is lovely. I guess what I mean is that I've been working in churches and in ministry for about a decade. I'm not working now and I want to find somewhere good to serve for a little while. I think that I need to do something different, but not too different." Wow, her technique was great; perhaps she should be a therapist. "I guess I have been a little at a loss."

Indeed, I was at a loss. Why wasn't this woman showing me the door? I was blathering on like an idiot. Nobody in their right mind would hire me with all this chatter. The more I thought about it, I realized that perhaps this was why I wasn't having much success with my job interviews lately.

At that point, I finally stopped and plastered a smile on my face, awaiting my dismissal from her office and possibly my banning from the building. I don't know what I was thinking. Why was I sitting in this woman's office trying to ascertain if she had possibly participated in a murder? What was the point of this? Shouldn't I be at home, in my orange sweatpants, minding my business?

Suddenly, she smiled, revealing some prominent canines. Her look shook me from reflection. She nodded.

"Your mom is Margaret Reed, right?" I nodded. Great, not only was I talking to this woman for no other reason than to discover that if she was a murderer, but now I find out she knows my mother. Did everyone know my mother? This was getting desperate and embarrassing. That was it, no more *Law and Order*, no more Jana Deleon mystery books and no more visiting Louise.

"I knew you looked familiar. I love your mom. She told you to speak with me, didn't she? She and I talk all the time. She told me how you totally got screwed in your former position. Look, we don't have any full-time positions here." She lifted my resumé and read off my degrees and some of my work history. Her eyes widened. I think she was impressed. That surprised and pleased me. She continued, "Frankly, most of the work here right now actually requires more physical than intellectual skills."

I blurted out, "I'm ready and willing to do anything to work right now!" I was practically begging for a position. Did I really want to work there? I thought I was just doing this in order to investigate, but I realized that I didn't want to hear another rejection. Ms. Cramer again examined my resumé and she put the paper on her desk.

"Our activities director needs an extra set of hands. If you can lift at least 20 lbs., pass a drug test and police background check, the position is yours."

I blinked and nodded. She reached across the desk and shook my hand. What had happened? Was this happening? Was I really going to take this job? Was I really going to investigate thefts and murder?

I left Ms. Cramer's office in a daze. The receptionist handed me a folder with the Riverview logo emblazoned on the cover. I thanked her and abruptly turned from the reception desk, feeling a little ill. When I turned, I saw him again, the sexy aide! He nodded at me. I fled to the closest restroom and threw up.

CHAPTER 9

"You got a job?" my mother asked suspiciously. I just nodded and smiled. I really didn't want to get into it. Somehow, I knew we would have to get into it.

I immediately sat at the kitchen table and hunched over my laptop. Why didn't the Wi-Fi work faster? I needed to look up a little more about this Tina Moore. I also needed to look up how to do my new found job. Maybe I would look up this Ms. Cramer, but somehow I doubted I would find a criminal background.

Aah, at last the Wi-Fi was working. Tina Moore's Facebook page came up first. The page was filled with comments offering sympathy for her death. Her picture was cheerful. A young woman in light blue scrubs held her twin boys. She smiled at the camera. I scrolled through some of her earlier posts. All were positive, either pictures of her boys, some selfies, but mostly reflecting on enjoying the people she served at Riverview. That was how she phrased what she did, she *served*.

"Did you hear me, Denise?" My mother scowled at me. She clicked her tongue and continued, "I said: Where is your new job?" I looked at my mother. Somehow she seemed to already know, but she craned her head forward, awaiting my reply.

"At Riverview." I looked back at the screen. I attempted to pull up Ms. Cramer on Facebook. I wracked my brain trying to remember Ms. Cramer's first name. Was it Lisa?

"Doing what?" She crossed her arms over her chest. She was suspicious, but I could also sense a little bit of excitement within her. Perhaps her daughter would eventually be working again.

"I'm going to be part-time assistant to the activities director. It's $11 an hour, 20 hours a week. After 6 months, I can get partial health insurance and pension, in addition to Social Security." I parroted back what Ms. Cramer had so elegantly explained.

My mom pursed her lips and sucked in her breath. I could almost see the words that my mom wanted to form. She had questions: Did I really want to do this? Shouldn't I be doing something more clerical or professional or serious? After all, I had two degrees. To her credit, she held her lips together.

"I met Ms. Cramer. She said she just loved you, Mom." My mother went to open her mouth, but stopped and cocked her head to the side, "you said I should get a job." She released a breath she was holding and the corners of her mouth turned up.

"At least it will get you out of the house, I guess," she said.

CHAPTER 10

Something about getting a job, even if it is only to investigate a murder, can fill a person with much needed pride. I would start work on Thursday at 9 a.m. My afternoon was spent filling out the copious paperwork for Riverview at the coffee shop before picking up my daughter early from daycare. We immediately headed to the playground at Audubon Park.

We stopped first at the fountain in front of the park. Emily loved to touch the water and splash. She circled it and then moved towards the flowers. She followed whatever caught her eye. At last, the playground caught her sight and she took off for the swings.

I followed at a short distance. I parked myself on a bench under a magnificent live oak and watched Emily swing. She had only recently discovered the joy of pumping. The weather was just about perfect for an October afternoon. Finally you could sit without sweating. I slipped off my blue cardigan, letting some sun on my shoulders and stretched my legs in front of me.

The park was still busy with runners, walkers and cyclists trying to get in some exercise before sunset. My eyes followed them as they made their way around the park. I really needed to start exercising more again. Frankly, I just needed to start exercising.

"Look, Mommy!" I looked back at Emily and beamed at her as she swung higher and higher, brown ponytail flying. I contemplated taking her for ice cream after I pried her off a swing—until I saw him.

Where had I seen him before? Riverview! The aide from Riverview leisurely jogged along the path. I could not take my eyes from him. I was mesmerized by the sweat glistening on his smooth head and six pack abs. He moved effortlessly with long strides and he wore some of the shortest possible running shorts I'd seen. Suddenly, October seemed July hot.

At this point, he looked straight at me. I turned my head and started whistling. I really hope he hadn't seen me ogling him.

"Mommy, why are you whistling? I want to play." Emily jumped off her swing and grabbed my hand, ready to join in a whistling game. How would I answer? Why was I whistling? Who was I kidding? I knew why I was whistling.

I smiled down at Emily, happy for a distraction from fantasies involving sweaty joggers who were soon to be co-workers while I tried to figure out who might have murdered Tina. I looked up to see if he had gone, only to discover that he had stopped running and was walking toward Emily and me.

"Hey, I've seen you at Riverview." He moved closer, extending his right hand. Still, feeling a little foolish for staring, I shook his hand.

"Yes, I've been at Riverview a lot lately. I thought that I recognized you. My name is Denise." I tried to sound confident and keep my eyes from creeping down his body. Unfortunately, his eyes were amazing. Who has grey, green and hazel eyes all at the same time? Also, how was it possible that he wasn't huffing and puffing after running?

"Yeah, you visit with Ms. Butler? She's a character. What do y'all talk about?" I just held his stare and I tried to remove my hand from his. He held a little too tightly before releasing it. I couldn't tell if he was just asking or being threatening. I think he probably enjoyed someone not being sure what his intention was. I was amazed at how much that both annoyed and frightened me.

"Sorry," he said, but he definitely didn't want to let go of my hand. He tried smiling at me, but the smile was fake. Emily pulled on my left hand. I looked down at her and back at him.

"I better go." I immediately headed for our car, pulling Emily into my arms. She looked over my shoulder at the man and waved. I looked back as he just stood there.

He waved back and said: "See you on Thursday."

I tried to move quickly, not running, but walking faster to the car. I was not going to be intimidated even if my legs felt like jelly. I put Emily in her car seat, got in and locked the door. I started the engine and turned on the heat. I was chilled. I'd forgotten my sweater.

I looked back at the park. The sun was beginning to set and made the great oak look menacing. As much as I hated to leave my sweater behind, I drove home.

CHAPTER 11

As far as first days go, Thursday started uneventfully. I agonized more about what I would wear than anything else that day, settling on dark slacks and a grey sweater set. When I first arrived, Ms. Cramer took me on the fastest tour of a seven-story building I'd ever been on. I think I timed her at 25 minutes. The next part of the morning at Riverview, I clicked through a computer program that taught the philosophy and regulations of Riverview. After three hours of videos and mouse clicks, I met with Alicia, the activities director, to go over the weekly schedule and her expectations of me. Although this day I would stay until 5, I was expected to come every day for four hours in the mornings. I was to get the different activity rooms ready for each event, call and remind speakers or activity leaders about their event, escort residents to events, fill out attendance forms, and then be present for those activities as an extra set of hands.

Around 12 I was starving. I helped Alicia set up a room for Tai Chi after lunch and then headed towards the cafeteria. The dining room was elegantly decorated with white table cloths and wait staff in blazers. The host stopped me at the doorway and directed me to the employee break room, two doors down from the cafeteria, next to a utility room.

I made my way to the tiny windowless room. I was kicking myself for forgetting my lunch as I looked through the snack machines. As fancy as Riverview was, you'd think they could spring for name-brand snacks in their machines, especially when they were charging almost $2 each.

"Hey, Denise!" I turned toward the voice and there was the aide, again. I think he must have sensed my unease. "I didn't mean to startle you. You forgot your sweater yesterday." He made it sound like I'd left my sweater on the floor of his bedroom or, at least, that's how I heard it. He held out my blue cardigan.

I went to reach for the sweater and he pulled his arm closer to him. He smirked at the gesture. If this guy was coming on to me, he was taking the creepiest approach possible. I just stared back, hoping my face didn't reveal my discomfort. What was this guy's problem?

I guess my stony demeanor worked because he handed me my sweater and looked down before saying: "Sorry." I've used the same technique on my daughter. I turned to the snack machine and looked for my selection.

"My name is Jason," he said. After all my earlier fantasies, I could barely contain my laughter.

"Really?" The word slipped out of my mouth before I could stop myself. He looked at me with an expression of confusion.

"What?" He cocked his head to the side and somehow I was no longer intimidated. Sure, he might be a muscle bound jerk face, but he didn't look threatening with his head turned on its side like a dog. He was genuinely perplexed.

"Nothing; you reminded me of someone." I coughed to control my giggles. With my newfound bravado, I pushed forward: "Why did you ask me about Ms. Butler on Tuesday?"

"Just curious, I guess," Jason said and shrugged. Somehow he didn't look like the type to be curious about anything, except maybe weights and fast cars.

"I didn't mean to bother you," he added and with that, he turned and moved toward the door. Now I was perplexed. What did he want? What might he know? Perhaps he could give me some insight into what went on behind the scenes at Riverview and it would be nice to keep looking at him.

"Wait, you didn't bother me!" He stopped and turned around. I closed the distance between us. "How long have you worked here at Riverview?"

A smile stretched across his face: "Why do you want to know?"

"Just curious, I guess." I was smooth. Yes, Denise is one smooth chick. I waited for his reply. He smiled and invited me to sit with him at one of the tables.

"Aren't you going to eat anything?" He placed his thermos on the table, opened it, and poured some sort of green concoction into the top of the thermos. I just stared.

"Not anymore." He laughed when I said that. If I'd had this type of timing a few months ago, I might still be a youth minister. Heck, if I could've had this timing when I was in college, I might have dated a ton of hotties. "So, have you worked here long? I started today."

"I started a few weeks back," he said. I waited for him to go on, but he proceeded to drink the green goo.

"Do you like it?" I asked. He shrugged looking at his thermos. "I mean working here," I added. I wracked my brain for any question that would require more than a "yes" or "no." Two men and a woman sat down at the other end of the table. The three were noisy. I knew that my window of serious conversation was closing quickly.

He turned his attention to the two men at the other end of the table: "You going to Wally's?" The other men nodded and he returned his attention to me, "What did you say?" I was losing this man's attention.

"Nothing. I was wondering what you do here." I wanted to roll my eyes.

"CNA." I was going to need pliers to get any information from this guy. I needed to think of something before he finished his awful drink and walked out. I felt like I was speed dating and needed to come up with something to keep his attention. Perhaps I could flash him, but I think that might have made him leave faster.

"Are you from New Orleans?" I can talk a hungry dog off a meat truck, but I really stink at small talk. I would give it a shot.

"Yes." Oh my God! Was he really just going to give one word answers?

"Have any brothers or sisters?" Ah ha! He would have to answer at least two words to this question. He sipped his concoction and I tried to keep control of my weak gag reflex.

"One brother." I got two words. I shook my head. I was floundering. I was not going to make it as an investigator at this rate.

"Know any good knock-knock jokes?" I asked quickly. That caught his attention.

"Is there such a thing as a good knock-knock joke?" he asked me back.

"Obviously, you've never heard the one about the banana." I said matter of fact. I know that Emily would agree with me. I stopped myself. He was definitely asking a rhetorical question. He was being funny. He looked like he was about to spit his green drink trying to control his laughter.

"You really need to warn me before you make a joke." He coughed and then took another sip. "Especially when I'm drinking something." The others at the end of the table stared at us and then returned to their discussion.

"I'll keep that in mind. What did you do before you worked here?" I knew as soon as I'd asked that I'd stepped over some invisible line. He stopped drinking and looked at me, assessing if he could trust me. He glanced momentarily at the trio at the end of the table. One of the men pounded the table and laughed telling a joke.

"This and that, not much." Apparently I came up short in his assessment. Why wouldn't he tell me? "What about you? What did you do?" I was not ready for his question.

I released a sigh I must have been holding since the beginning of our conversation. He laughed in reply. "I worked at a church as coordinator of youth and young family ministries," I answered.

"That's different," he replied.

"Yes, it is different from here." We both nodded. We were quiet again. He finished drinking, wiped his upper lip with the back of his hand, and stood up.

"It was nice sitting with you, Denise. I'll see you around." I shook my head in agreement and waved as he walked away. He lightly punched the man at the end of the table. At least I had my sweater.

CHAPTER 12

The rest of the day sped by with Tai Chi, then Bingo, followed by afternoon Bible Study. At Tai Chi, I might have pulled a muscle in my thigh, but I pushed forward. Certainly if a 90-year-old could finish the class, I could as well. During Bingo I managed to win once. The prize was Tiger Balm. I considered that pretty lucky. After Bible Study, I had a little time before I could leave and I made my way to Ms. Butler's room. I thought I would check in on her. I wanted to tell her that I got the position. I knocked quietly, and the door swung open.

"Denise! I heard from Toots that you came back. I knew you would get the job." I wracked my brain trying to remember when I'd seen Toots today, but I figured that Riverview, like many small communities, probably ran on gossip. I just smiled and she shooed me into her suite. She directed me to a chintz love seat. I sat.

"Would you like something to drink? I have sherry! We should celebrate your new position." Before I could say anything, she ran into the other room and produced two already filled glasses. She handed me a glass. We clinked glasses and she slammed down her sherry as I sipped. We talked about my new position and responsibilities.

"Denise, this is going to be the first step of rebuilding that confidence of yours." She pointed at me and beamed proudly. "Just think, you didn't even want the job, and they hired you. That's how great you are." I blushed and tried to deflect her compliment, but she went on, "Denise, you're too old to turn down a compliment and diminish your worth. That will be one of the best lessons you can teach your child; learn it now. Say thank you, damnit."

"Thank you, Louise," I dutifully replied. I sipped the sherry again and shook my head.

"So, what have you found out so far?" She settled back in her chair and propped the sherry on the arm of the chair, awaiting my reply.

"I found out where the cafeteria is." I smiled at Ms. Butler and sipped more sherry. I just didn't know how she could drink this stuff. Ms. Butler shifted a little to the left in her wingback chair and crossed her legs. I could see she was rolling her eyes behind her huge glasses. She was disappointed.

"I know where the cafeteria is, Denise. I live here." She grumbled. "I meant: what have you found out about our investigation?" She leaned forward and focused on me. She rubbed her hands together.

"I saw Ms. Cramer on Tuesday, and I spoke with her just to get a feel about her. I cannot tell anything. She has an outrageous fashion sense." I thought about Ms. Cramer's suit. She did look good, even if she was out there. I looked down at my own outfit. Maybe she would give me some pointers?

"Tell me about it," Louise replied. Her gaze pleaded that I continue.

Louise sucked in and bit her lip. I went on: "She cannot be all bad. She gave me this job." Really, Ms. Cramer had seemed pretty nice. She was maybe a little cold, but she was professional.

Louise sipped her sherry. "I guess she did. Of course, I knew you would get it." I wondered how she could be so sure about that when I was convinced I'd never be gainfully employed again. She continued,

"Surely, you found out something else today?" She moved back to the edge of her seat, focusing her attention on me.

"Well, I spoke with Jason. He's a CNA." Louise looked confused. She had no idea who I was talking about. "The super-hot guy whose scrubs are going to split because of his muscles?" I noticed that her cheeks looked a little pink.

Louise raised her eyebrow. "Oh yes, I'm familiar with the young gentleman—nice buns—but what does this stud have to do with the investigation?" She sipped her sherry, licking her lips. Her expression was a mix of wishfulness and mischievousness.

"Uh, a few days ago, I ran into him at the park, and he asked me what you and I were meeting about. So I asked him why he asked, but he didn't give much of an answer and then he was kind of mysterious about his former job." That caught Louise's interest.

"What did he used to do?" Louise asked, tapping her fingers on the side of her glass. She was getting frustrated.

"That's what I mean. He wouldn't say. What do you think? Does he know something about what's going on?" Louise thought about my questions for a moment, again tapping her glass.

"I don't think so. He's pretty new, really the last few weeks. Of course, it might not hurt to keep an eye on him," Louise said with a wink. We both giggled. "I have an idea, Denise. Are you available tomorrow at 6?" Louise tapped her fingers on her crystal glass.

"Well, it is short notice; I would need someone to watch Emily. What do you want to do?"

"Denise, I'm going to throw a party, and you are the guest of honor! While you're there, you can ask some questions and get some clues." She immediately put down her glass and picked up her cellphone on the table. She furiously began texting.

"What are you doing?" She held the device close to her face.

"I'm texting. I'm old, but I am still hip," she said from behind the phone.

"Who are you texting?" I couldn't imagine who.

"I have to invite some friends, and I'm going to invite Ms. Cramer." She said the woman's name with disgust. "Of course, I'll probably have to call her. She's no good at texting. I'll mention it to some of the staff as well."

"Is this a good idea, Louise?" I asked. I felt unsure. I hadn't been to a party in months. I also wasn't sure how I'd go about asking people questions about thefts at Riverview.

"Did you have plans?" she asked, peering over the top of her glasses while she texted. She knew the answer before she asked. I gulped my sherry. "I didn't think so. While we are at it, let's invite your mother!" I took another swig of sherry.

CHAPTER 13

I rode up the elevators to the top floor of Riverview, looking at my reflection in the elevator doors. I was wearing my midnight blue silk blouse and pencil skirt. Despite gaining some weight, I still looked pretty good tonight. I'd let my hair down, and I have to admit that after a good wash and blow dry, my hair look glossy. I pulled out my lipstick to reapply when the doors opened. I was immediately greeted by Louise, who linked her arm through mine. Louise looked lovely in a grey dress. Pinned to her dress was a broach that was a cluster of freshwater pearls set in silver.

We both admired each other and exchanged compliments. "Where's your mom this evening?" Louise led me down the hallway to the "party room," as she called it.

"She decided to watch Emily for me. She thought I needed to get out." I'd left Emily and Mom at home in pajamas, eating ravioli and watching *Daniel Tiger*. Mom promised that Emily would only have one more cookie, but I suspected that would not be the case. Of course, it was Friday night.

We giggled as we walked down the hallway. Louise again complimented my choice in blouses. She began to fill me in on the individuals I would see at the party. The group was small. She described each resident and what item they were missing and suspect had been stolen.

As we approached the end of the hall, I was expecting to enter a room a lot like the dining room, but discovered that the "party room" was actually a beautiful atrium and deck that overlooked Audubon Park. The room was awash in orange and pink from the setting sun.

There were about 15 or 20 people in the room. They were broken into a few smaller groups gathered around the table. Some held wine glasses and others held little plates. I recognized Nolan and his friend Toots, Ms. Cramer and a few of the residents. Alicia was chatting in a corner with two or three members of the staff, while nibbling on a cracker. One of them was Melinda, who I'd met briefly. She worked in housekeeping. I couldn't recognize the other because his back was to me.

In the middle of the room was a circular table with a couple of platters of cheese and crackers, vegetables and a cake. My stomach grumbled with delight. I gravitated to the cake, but Louise gripped my arm and led me towards Ms. Cramer.

"Get ready, Denise." I looked down at the woman at my side. She suddenly transformed from the vital, lively woman I'd been visiting for the last couple of weeks to the feeble old woman who'd mistaken me for Tina at the church service. What was going on?

"Hello, Ms. Cramer," Louise croaked out the words. "I want to thank you for hiring Denise. She is just lovely." Louise reached out with her free hand and gripped Ms. Cramer's arm. I could tell that she was holding her too tightly. The two women examined each other. This evening, Ms. Cramer had chosen to wear a silky grey pant suit with a neon pink lining and matching pink pumps. "Nice suit," said Louise, raising her eyebrows.

Ms. Cramer's smile stretched so much that it looked like it hurt. Apparently, Ms. Cramer didn't care for Louise any more than Louise cared for her. I could tell that she was uncomfortable with Louise holding her arm.

"Of course, Ms. Butler, we're thrilled that Denise has joined us at Riverview. What a wonderful addition." Ms. Cramer nodded her head at me. "You know that her mother is Margaret Reed." I felt like I was being described like a piece of furniture, and Ms. Cramer was proud of her acquisition. I watched as she tried to extract her arm from Louise's grip.

"Yes, Margaret. She is such a gift to Tuesday morning worship. She practically knows all of New Orleans. A fine business woman, a debutante with a heart of gold. I guess the saying is true: the apple doesn't fall far from the tree." Louise gave my arm a tender squeeze. I was surprised that Louise had quoted an article written long ago about my mother and her time helping in the Junior League. *How could she remember that?* I wondered. Of course the quotation was pretty well known and Louise did read the paper every day. Louise continued to prattle on, "Denise is just so sweet. She reminds me of that Tina girl. Doesn't she remind you of Tina, Ms. Cramer?" Louise went on. "Whatever happened to Tina?" Louise tapped her chin in faux puzzlement.

If looks could kill, I believe that I would have been scraping Louise off the floor. Ms. Cramer glared at Louise, oblivious to my being there. To Ms. Cramer's credit, she maintained her composure. "Well, what a beautiful broach, Ms. Butler." She reached out to touch the jewelry, but Louise stepped back to avoid her touch.

"Thank you for noticing, Ms. Cramer. Tina liked this broach too. Whatever happened to her?" Louise continued her attack. Her gaze fixed on Ms. Cramer, like a predator observing prey.

Ms. Cramer answered through a clenched smile: "Tina is dead, Ms. Butler. Don't you remember? She had a terrible accident. Really too bad, actually; she was a nice girl." She paused before saying that Tina was a nice girl, as if grudgingly admitting something. "Yes, Tina died in a terrible accident. Accidents can happen at any time and anywhere." Something about the way that Ms. Cramer said her last sentence sounded like a threat, but I couldn't be sure that I wasn't letting my imagination run wild.

The air between the two women was growing thick. The two locked in on each other. Had we been in a bar, Louise and Ms. Cramer might have come to blows. What was Louise trying to do?

One by one, residents and a couple of staff members moved closer to the conversation, like spectators at an accident. The group became quiet and it was clear that everyone was listening to the exchange. Ms. Cramer looked at me and quickly switched her tone: "How have your first two days been, Denise?"

Before I could answer, Louise continued: "How goes your investigation into those thefts, Ms. Cramer? Are you investigating?" Ms. Cramer's face turned crimson, but she held the smile. She was not going to say anything more.

I took the cue and jumped in, attempting to seem oblivious to the *tête à tête* I'd just witnessed: "It has been just wonderful, Ms. Cramer. I cannot thank you enough for giving me this job. I'm enjoying myself and meeting so many interesting people." I smiled as sincerely as possible.

Ms. Cramer just answered, "I'm sure. Would you excuse me, Denise, Ms. Butler?" With that, Ms. Cramer made a beeline for the elevators. The group began to murmur and laugh with her exit, like the Wicked Witch had left Munchkin Village.

I turned to Louise. "What did you think you were doing?" Louise had been about as subtle with Ms. Cramer as a Las Vegas showgirl.

Louise gave me a look of innocence: "I was just making conversation. That's what I do. Come on, I want you to speak with everyone here." With that, she ended our conversation and began introducing me to each resident.

By the end of the evening, I'd spoken with the other party guests. Louise deftly brought up the topic of the thefts with each one, and all of them shared their stories. Some were missing jewelry, some cash, and some had just noticed that things had been moved around their rooms. Each item was something rather small.

As I listened, I wondered how many might have just misplaced an item, but each one had a story of something missing. No one seemed senile and the items tended to be something that one would put in the same place again and again solely to keep from losing.

It certainly seemed that there was a thief or thieves at Riverview, but how would one track them down? I thought that perhaps if someone *was* stealing, maybe they were targeting a certain floor or area, so I also asked where they lived in Riverview. However, all these residents were all spread throughout floors and on different hallways.

I tried to make conversation with individual members of staff at the reception, but as I would approach, they moved away, mostly congregating around Alicia. I saw the man who'd been speaking with Alicia earlier. I finally recognized him as one of the men who'd sat with Jason and me on my first day at lunch. I still didn't know his name.

I felt like a 7th grader looking for a seat in the cafeteria. I arrived at the group and they scattered like cockroaches when you turn on a light. It did nothing for my self-esteem. Two women moved to the snack table and furiously began picking up, another man walked over to the lone garbage can and picked it up and carried it out the door. I was left with Alicia.

"This was nice." Alicia smiled, slipping her hand into the pocket of her pink smock to grab something. I smiled back at her. She rocked nervously on her heels and popped something into her mouth from her pocket.

"Yes, this was nice. I really like working here with you, Alicia," I told her. She smiled sweetly at me, like a child receiving a present. Actually, I did like working with her. As supervisors go, Alicia was great. She told you exactly what she wanted, showed you how to do things, helped, and then would leave you alone. Even if I might have only pursued this job on a crazy whim, I was enjoying my time at Riverview, so far.

Toots and his pal Nolan slipped over to either side of me. Toots attempted to whisper: "How's your investigation going?" The room once again grew quiet. Nolan nodded in anticipation of my response. Alicia looked quizzically at me, pushing a loose strand of brown hair behind her ear.

I gently held Toots' arm and turned and stepped away from Alicia. I laughed nervously, "What?" I realized as soon as I spoke the question that I should have shut up because Toots began to repeat his question so loudly that anyone in the lobby would hear him. Louise gave him a sharp elbow to the stomach. Nolan took the cue and scurried away in the opposite direction, but Toots missed the subtlety.

"Why'd you do that, Louise? Is she investigating the thefts or not? I'm just asking a question." Toots rubbed his midsection and looked indignant. Louise grabbed his arm in what I could only imagine was a vice grip.

"Looks like you've had too much to drink, Harold. Walk with me," she practically growled the words. So his real name was Harold; who knew? The two walked to one of the windows. The lamp posts in the park were turning on. The group returned to their chatter and one by one made their exits. I turned toward Alicia to see her scurry from the room.

I made my way, at last, to the snack table. I hoped that at least one slice of cake remained, but the group must have been vultures. The staff was already whisking away whatever remained. I felt a soft tap on my shoulder and turned around.

"Excuse me, I don't think that I've had the opportunity to meet you yet. I'm Doctor Martin." A brown-eyed Adonis shook my hand. The man was completely perfect—brown hair with just a touch of grey at the temples, brown dreamy eyes, neatly pressed navy suit, and expensive shoes. He was every bit the CEO.

"My name is Denise Reed. I am the new assistant to the activities director." I smiled brightly. Even if I never figured out who was stealing at Riverview, perhaps I had found my new husband? He smiled, flashing some of the best caps I've seen in a really long time.

"Denise Reed? Is your mother Margaret?" I nodded. Of course he knew my mother. "She sold me my house a few years ago. What a quality lady! You know how hard that is to find?" I was not sure how to take the compliment or if it even was a compliment.

"Thank you. I'll tell her that you said so." I would just take the message and let my mom interpret it at her leisure.

"She just looked and looked for me. I was married at the time and the wife could never be satisfied." His face tightened as he remembered. "Never be satisfied with anything. Never enough bathrooms, too many bedrooms, no crown molding…" I sensed that he relived this episode in his life often and he probably needed to share his frustrations about his ex-wife with a therapist.

I thought that it might be best to interrupt him, but before I could get a word out, Jason appeared at Dr. Martin's side, "Dr. Martin I need to speak with you about something." Dr. Martin sighed heavily. Jason didn't even look at me. I was surprised at how disappointed I was. It looked like Dr. Martin was a bust as next husband material.

"Would you excuse me, Ms. Reed?" With that, the two men walked out the room. The room was emptying, the snack table was cleared. I waited for a bit, unsure where Louise had wandered off to with Harold. Was she coming back? Would we regroup? I looked at my watch and decided that I needed to call it a night. I walked down the hall to the elevator and pressed the button.

I guess the night was pretty good. I had dressed up, gone to a party, questioned people about stolen property and almost flirted with a doctor. All in all, this Friday night was looking a lot better than most Friday nights. The elevator doors opened and I stepped in.

I stepped in and leaned against the back of the elevator. I pressed the button for the lobby. Before the doors closed, a hand shot between the doors. The doors opened, revealing Jason. Without a word, he entered the elevator and pressed the lobby button. We rode down in silence. The elevator slowed as it reached the first floor. Before the doors opened, Jason turned and spoke: "You look really pretty this evening."

With that, he bolted through the doors and disappeared into the lobby, but not before making my night.

CHAPTER 14

I got in my car and looked in my visor mirror. I did look good, and it was too early to head home. I wracked my brain about where I could go. As I waited for the electric gate to open, a rap on my window startled me. I looked through the window at Jason.

I rolled down the window and he asked: "Would you like to grab a drink?" Perhaps my evening was going to get even better?

"Absolutely!" I practically shouted the word. I looked good, but I still had no game.

"Let's meet at Wally's on Carrollton." I knew the place from my younger years. Not really a quiet, "let's meet for a romantic drink," kind of place, but I didn't have any other plans for the evening.

Because it was early in the evening, one could still find a table. I remembered the bar from high school because it was actually impossible to get in and therefore popular with Tulane upperclassmen. I made my way to the counter and bought my white wine and then moved through the light crowd to a table in a corner.

I waited for Jason to arrive. I crossed my legs and tried to arrange myself to seem more alluring; instead I kept slipping from my chair. Finally, I saw Jason enter and head straight to the bar. When he had his drink, he headed my way.

He moved confidently through the crowd. I watched as other women in the room followed his movements with their eyes. In jeans and a long sleeve shirt, he oozed casual. He chose a seat right next to me. I could smell his cologne or shampoo; whatever it was, it smelled like mint and leather.

"Not drinking some seaweed or some other green drink?" I asked, hoping to break the ice. He just looked at me as he took a sip of his Guinness. His forehead wrinkled in thought. Wow, he looked great in thought.

He put his drink on the table and gazed at me. I felt like his eyes moved up and down my body. I returned the stare, taking in pretty much every inch of his body. I cannot say that he came up lacking, but I couldn't help but feel self-conscious. It had been a very long time since I'd had a drink with a man and an even longer time since I'd felt that I looked sexy.

"You're funny," he said. I got that a lot in my life, along with "and you're smart." I got that a lot as well. At this moment, I would have preferred: "You are a goddess and I want to kiss you here and until the end of time." I was disappointed.

"Thank you," I answered. I sipped my white wine and looked around the room. This was going to be agony. I was sitting next to one of the hottest men I'd ever seen and he thought I was funny. These last few months just got better. What had happened to me looking pretty?

"I say that because I was wondering what you're doing at Riverview." His tone was deadly serious. Usually, the man seemed so easy going.

I took a gulp of my wine: "What do you mean?" I tried to seem casual, but I wasn't pulling off this look. I straightened in my chair and leaned toward him, wondering if perhaps I'd misunderstood his question.

"As far as I can tell, you're a glorified assistant camp counselor for old folks. What are you doing at Riverview?" The description stung. I thought that while the position was pretty small, at least I was helping people. I was utterly flummoxed. I was not going to sit here and be insulted by this testosterone-filled stud muffin.

I put down my glass, and made a point of looking him up and down. I crossed my arms: "What is that supposed to mean? What are *you* doing at Riverview?"

He lifted his hands in mock surrender. "I didn't mean to insult you. What I'm saying is that you seem too smart and too classy to be working there, especially in a part-time position. I'm a CNA; of course I'd work there."

"Well, you don't look much like a CNA," I said. Yep, that was the best I could come up with at the moment. I let out a huff.

"What's that supposed to mean?" he asked, and I just shrugged. Yes, I match wits with the best of them. I sipped my wine and we sat in silence. A smile creeped across his face when he realized what I'd implied. "I like to work out."

"I'm sure." I was mentally kicking myself now for making the comment. I scanned the room, avoiding eye contact. I crossed my legs and focused on a blinking Budweiser sign behind the bar. The neon light was irritating so I returned to looking at him.

"I have a theory why you're at Riverview. I think you're at Riverview because you're helping Ms. Butler investigate something, maybe those thefts. Am I right?" I was stunned that he knew exactly why I was at Riverview. How had he figured that out?

"What if I am?" I asked. He shifted in his chair and stretched out long, lean legs in front of him. He swallowed some of his beer, wiping his hand across his mouth.

"I think that would be foolish for someone as smart as you. I think it might be dangerous too, especially for someone who has no idea what she's doing." He spoke quietly, staring at me like he was drilling a hole in my head. I was completely taken aback by these questions.

"How do you know that I don't know what I'm doing?" Certainly I knew that I had no clue what I was doing, but it couldn't have been that obvious. Right? "Also, isn't it only dangerous if something is really happening at Riverview?" I shot back.

"That's how I know that you don't know what you're doing. Something is always happening. If you go poking around, you might find something and you won't like it." A chill went down my spine. I finished my wine.

I stood up and looked down at him, hoping he was not looking at my double chin. "It was nice having a drink with you," I lied. I went to leave and he reached out and touched my arm. I looked back at him.

"You need to be careful, okay?" He softly stroked my arm. He gave me goose bumps, but I didn't want him to stop. His beautiful light eyes gazed at me.

I opened my mouth to say something, but the words stopped in my throat. I was struck with the kindness in his words and the tenderness in his touch, even if he was trying to warn me away from investigating Riverview. I guess he wasn't really a muscle-bound jerk face after all. Maybe he was a friend.

CHAPTER 15

My weekend was quiet. All night long, I dreamed of stacking chairs in the activity room at Riverview while Jason jogged back and forth down the hall in a speedo. I would wake up and turn over and then I'd once again dream about something else at Riverview. Finally, Saturday morning arrived.

Emily climbed into bed with me and chirped: "Can we go to the muffin place?" She was talking about P.J's on Magazine. I thought her idea was brilliant and we wandered down to the neighborhood coffee shop. After purchasing Emily's chocolate muffin and chocolate milk and my café latte, we chose an iron table and two chairs and sat outside on Magazine Street. It was still early, so there was not much traffic, just people walking their dogs or joggers.

I'd just opened my newspaper when I heard a familiar voice, "Denise Reed, where have you been hiding?" I looked up into the large smile of my high school friend, Carrie Boudreaux. Carrie looked radiant even in workout clothes. Her usually wavy light brown hair was pulled back in a simple ponytail, a slight sweat glistening on her perfectly freckled skin.

I almost burst into tears seeing her. I was so happy. For months I'd been hiding out from friends, embarrassed about not working. I guess I was worried what they would say, but that self-consciousness melted the moment I saw my friend.

She immediately hugged me, scooped up Emily and sat down with her on her lap. "Denise, I've been missing you. Where have you been?" She waited for my reply.

I raised my eyebrows and smiled sheepishly: "I lost my job at St. Christopher's. I've been trying to figure out what to do next." I just blurted it out. With Carrie, I could always tell her anything. For that matter, I probably couldn't keep anything from her for very long.

"Oh, Denise, I'm sorry. That totally sucks. I heard something like that. But, weren't you kind of ready for a move? You didn't really like your boss that much either." I swear that Carrie remembered everything. It was probably the reason she was a brilliant attorney.

"I know, but...." I didn't need to finish my sentence. She nodded. She understood that even if I didn't like the position, it didn't mean that I wanted to be pushed out of it. *Of course, how does anyone ever get out of lousy positions, if something or someone doesn't push them?* I wondered

"Do you have any leads?" Carrie smiled with such enthusiasm. She caught me off guard with the question.

"What?" Was she asking about my investigation? How could she know about that?

"Do you have any job prospects?" she clarified. I wondered if I should tell her what I was doing at Riverview. Instead, I decided I'd just share that I'd started there.

"I found a position at Riverview. I'm working part time, with the activities coordinator." I shrugged and Denise nodded.

"That's a good place. Really pretty, at least the outside is." I nodded in agreement. She leaned back in her chair and announced dramatically, "Ooh, that's where I want to go when I die, I mean, when I'm old." We both laughed at her goof, but the words struck me. If she only knew what I was doing at Riverview, yikes!

"You know, Denise, that actually sounds like a great position. When are they going to make you full time?" she asked earnestly. I felt proud. I guess I had found a position, even if it was part-time. I couldn't believe how much better I was feeling about myself and my situation just sitting with Carrie.

For the next half hour, we chatted about her life, what was happening in her firm, possible and impossible boyfriends, her family and other class-mates. My cheeks hurt from laughing. Emily joined in on our laughter.

"Denise, you know when we were in high school and you said that you wanted to write a book?" I looked at Carrie. This topic certainly seemed to come from nowhere.

"Yes, of course; why do you ask?" Now Carrie looked unsure. Carrie never looked unsure. I wondered what she was thinking about. She shifted Emily on her lap.

"I wrote a screenplay. Would you help me with it? I need someone to—I don't know—look at it. I need someone who can help and someone I trust." Now that was unexpected.

"I would be honored," I replied. I lifted my mug in a toast. Carrie looked relieved. We both hashed out a schedule for when I'd start looking at her work. She told me the plot and about her characters. I felt excitement about this new project.

Finally, Emily began to squirm, so we both stood up to leave. Carrie hugged me and she headed across Magazine Street, toward Downtown. I watched her as she walked and noticed a couple walking on the other side of the street. They were Alicia, my supervisor, and the pimply-faced orderly from Riverview. Well, ooh-la-la!

I waved at her across the street. At first she didn't see me. She was caught up in some conversation with pimple face. She held his hand and nuzzled in to whisper something in his ear. He smirked. Then she turned and saw my wave. She smiled and waved back, but her pimply faced companion did not. The two walked into the other coffee shop on the corner. This was just a morning of meetings.

Emily and I leisurely wandered down Magazine, stopping to admire the toys in the window of one of the shops. Emily hopped back and forth, begging to go in, but thankfully they were closed. Finally, we walked to the Whole Foods and sampled some free samples of cheese, and then we slipped out the back door.

When we returned to the house, my mother cornered me. She had returned from her three-mile walk with Marilyn, her best friend. She blocked my path to my room. She was wearing her turquoise blue sweat suit and her usual pearls; for a woman who'd just finished a workout, she actually looked fresh, maybe a little flushed.

"Denise, you haven't talked much about your new job. How are things going?" I thought about dodging around her, but she looked entirely too pumped. She would probably just tackle me.

"Good, I guess," I answered honestly, if not fully. No need to tell the woman that I was investigating a crime or crimes. I could tell that she wasn't buying it.

"You guess?" She jumped on the words. "What is going on over there? What is it like?" She tapped her white New Balance-clad foot.

"It's a good place. They have lousy food in the vending machines, but the residents are nice. What do you want to know, Mom?" I wondered what she did want to know.

"Do you think it's possible for this to become full time?" In other words, was I ever going to be gainfully employed and not just marginally or unemployed forever?

"I guess it's possible." I shrugged my shoulders. My mother pursed her lips. She hated shrugging.

"Denise, I think that this could be a really good thing for you, if it could be full time. Please don't be lackadaisical about this. I know a lot of people who live and work there. I might want to move there in a few years." Oh, my gosh; she didn't want me to embarrass her—that was it. I immediately hugged her.

"I'll do my best, Mom. I don't know if it'll become full time or if it'll last, but I'll do my best." She looked at me as if she was unsure.

"Is there a discount for family members of employees?" she asked hopeful

CHAPTER 16

In the afternoon, I looked at my phone at another text from my former boss: "Would like to speak with you. When are you available?" I wondered what he might want. Was he going to beg me to take my job back? For that matter, did I want my old job back? I decided that my best course of action was to try to ignore it for now.

Try as I might to ignore the message, I thought about my time working at St. Christopher's. I'd loved the kids and spending time with them. I would lead youth group and play games. I would try to engage the parents and younger siblings in book and Bible studies. I was most proud of getting a small group together to start serving breakfast to the homeless once a week, but I always felt I was limited in what I was able to do. I wanted to do more, but if I'm completely honest, I'm not sure what that would have been. I was frustrated and wanted to be more than what my old boss would call "a glorified babysitter."

I had hated working for my old boss. Reverend Foucher would run either hot or cold. He would compliment you, and then in the next breath he'd crack a joke at your expense. He lamented that the church didn't do enough for the poor and then blow off my ideas for outreach as he drove away in his Mercedes. Most irritating was that I usually found myself at odds with him when I'd want to try something new. He would take my ideas and present them as his own. At the same time, everyone loved him.

I was tired of the politics in the position. I was tired of working for someone I didn't like. I was also tired of being a "glorified babysitter." I looked for another position at another church in town. I thought that I had the job in the bag. I suppose that I was foolish for even telling my old boss that I was looking for a change, especially when I didn't have a new position, but I told him anyway. And he gave me the boot or rather invited me to boot myself.

I looked at the message again. I was not sure that I *was* available. I deleted it.

CHAPTER 17

The rest of the weekend flew by with more playgrounds, more coffee, and more looking up how to investigate a crime on the internet. I discovered you should probably be pretty careful looking that up. You might not like what you find. I decided instead to stick to reading celebrity gossip and Facebook.

On Sunday, we headed to church and lunch at my older sister's house. Susan and I lazed on the couch as Emily and her cousins played in the front yard. We talked about the mysteries we were reading. She talked about her job and complained about her son's school. I talked about what I was doing at Riverview.

Susan nodded and asked, "What do they have you doing?"

"I told you, Susan, I'm helping the activity coordinator." I sipped my iced tea and stood up to stretch my legs before settling back down on her couch.

"That's not what I mean, Denise. What are you doing specifically? Changing bed pans? Rubbing ointment on someone's varicose veins?" The image that Susan created with her words made my stomach unsettled.

"No, we set up activities for the residents, like art class or Bingo. I escort people to and from activities. I help arrange the activities and the room." Susan nodded.

"They can't just get the orderlies to do that?"

"I guess they could, but a lot of time the aides or housekeeping staff are cleaning during the activities." We were both quiet for a bit.

"Denise, I'm glad that you're doing something, and it kind of sounds like a good fit." She smiled at me. We clinked our glasses in a toast. The rest of the weekend slipped away in barbecue, iced tea and finishing a Janet Evonovich novel. Late on Sunday afternoon, I received Carrie's email with her screenplay attached and started reading it. All and all, I had a good weekend.

CHAPTER 18

"I didn't know that you lived near me," Alicia
exclaimed while we moved chairs in the activity room,
preparing for the Monday morning drawing class with
Mr. Prater. We arranged the chairs in a circle with one
chair and small table in the center.

"I just live around the corner on Joseph Street.
Where are you?" I was surprised that Alicia even
remembered seeing me. I'd forgotten until she spoke.

"Tchoupitoulas. I love that area. Don't you? You can
walk anywhere. I love the coffee shops there. There are
so many really cute shops. I love Whole Foods," she
said the last bit with added emphasis. I nodded at Alicia
because everybody loved Whole Foods.

"Have you lived in the neighborhood long?" I asked.
I moved a large easel to the middle of the room.

"I moved there about three months ago. My
boyfriend and I moved in together. We found a pretty
small place, but so super cute." She inspected the easel
and moved it about an inch to the left. A dreamy
expression crossed her face, "We're going to get
married in June." Ah l'amour!

"That's wonderful, Alicia. I'm so happy for you. I
bet you're busy planning." Again, Alicia moved the
easel, and then she stepped back to examine it.

"We aren't doing anything big, been there and done
that." She waved her hand in front of her face like she
was swatting a fly in disgust. I understood a little
something about big weddings followed by big
disappointment. I thought back to my own several years

before. The ceremony had been beautiful, my dress was amazing and the food was fabulous, but a great big party still couldn't assuage my doubts that day. "We'll probably do something small, just family. We don't have a lot of money, so we're focusing on what's truly important." I nodded in agreement at her sentiment. She continued with total earnestness, "I'm saving for us to get married at Disney World. I'm going to do it the right way this time." She lost me on that one.

She promptly turned around and started pushing a table into the corner of the room. She moved with the energy of a small espresso-filled dog. Clearly, the woman did indeed love her coffee. She placed drawing pads on each of the chairs and continued chattering. Alicia spent an agonizing amount of time placing a bowl of wax fruit on the table in the middle. After turning it about 14 times, she stopped and stepped back. When the room was set-up, she clapped her hands.

"This looks just perfect." Alicia reached into her pocket and popped some small snack in her mouth. I noticed on the first day that Alicia always carried nuts or crackers with her in the pocket of the pink smock she wore. I marveled that a woman as slender as Alicia could snack as much as she did, but if I had half her energy, I, too, would probably need a snack to keep me going.

We headed down the hallway to gather the nine members of the class. I knocked on Lydia Shanks' door. When the door opened, I was looking at a real life version of Sophia Petrillo from *Golden Girls*. She excitedly spoke about the class as she gathered her pencils, shawl and other items. Lydia fumbled with her watch and at last took it off and put it in her bedroom. When she returned, she handed me her small bag, and I waited in the hallway.

Down the hallway, I saw Alicia's pimply-faced beau and I smiled at him. He just stared as he ran the vacuum cleaner over the pastel carpet in the hallway. Not the friendliest chap. At the other end of the hall, I noticed Jason escorting another resident to her room. He smiled down at the woman and she giggled. Obviously, he had that effect on every woman. For the briefest moment, he looked up at me and my heart skipped a beat.

At last, Lydia was ready for class and we walked to the activity room. When she was settled in there, she took her bag from me. I, then, went to collect my next class member. After each member had arrived or was escorted to the room, class began. The group began to draw a bowl of fruit under the careful eye of their teacher, Mr. Prater. The first thing he did was to rearrange the fruit in the bowl and then move the bowl.

I saw Alicia purse her lips. Alicia snacked in the corner of the room and held her own drawing pad. She rocked back and forth as she drew the fruit bowl. Mr. Prater wandered the room, looking at each student's work, commenting on some, adjusting pencils or answering questions. I took this moment to head to the bathroom. I wandered down the hallway, and as I passed Lydia's room, I saw the door was slightly open.

I knew that we had shut the door, but I didn't think too much of it because often the cleaning staff would step in and clean during activities. The staff would place a "cleaning" sign on the door knob as they worked. I guess someone had forgotten the sign this time. I moved a little closer to the room, listening for the telltale sound of a vacuum.

"Denise, do you have a minute?" I turned around to Ms. Cramer. She smiled at me and waved me toward her. I walked to her and smiled back. I felt like my eyes would start watering looking at her magenta suit with beige heels. The woman had some style sense—not sure what—but something was going on.

She motioned me to one of the sitting areas at the end of the hall with a small couch and two plush chairs. She sat on the couch and I sat on a chair across from her as she spoke: "I wanted to speak to you after Friday's event. I left kind of abruptly."

This time, I would just let her talk and see what emerged. She continued, "I had to leave kind of early, before I could give you a little context about Riverview. Ms. Butler is a sweet woman. She is particularly attached to some people, particularly a lovely young woman named Tina Moore. Poor Tina." Ms. Cramer looked up and pursed her lips, like she was trying to stop herself from crying. The way she spoke about Tina, one might think that she was referring to her old aunt and yet, I knew that Tina had been a young, lively mother, or at least her Facebook page alluded to it.

Ms. Cramer cooed, "Poor dear." She sounded ridiculous. Was she some gossipy character from a Jane Austin novel? She continued, speaking in a whisper "Poor Tina was in a terrible accident. She was hit by a car after work, waiting for her bus." I wasn't sure why she was telling me this. How did she want me to respond?

I waited and then spoke: "That's just terrible, Ms. Cramer. You must miss her so much. Were you two close?" I reached out and patted her hand on the arm of the couch. She snatched it away.

"No," Ms. Cramer shot back with irritation, obviously surprised by the question. She quickly recovered her composure and continued, "Yes, it was horrible. No, I was not close to Tina, but Ms. Butler was. I think that Ms. Butler is having a hard time dealing with the loss. I'm not sure that she can accept it, *and* accept that it was an accident. Frankly, I'm afraid that Ms. Butler doesn't care that much for me, so I'm not sure that I'm the best one to help her."

"I see." I would let her keep talking. Now things were getting interesting.

"I can tell that Ms. Butler really likes you, Denise. I think that you need to help her with her grief, really accept what has happened so she can heal. I hate to see one of our residents suffering. We are a family at Riverview." Ms. Cramer pressed her palms together as if in prayer and held them to her chin. She could not have looked less sincere. The movement and words smacked of manipulation, but not necessarily of malice. Also, wouldn't the chaplain be better suited to deal with someone's grief?

"Ms. Cramer, I would be happy to help Ms. Butler, but what happened to Tina Moore? What do you know about the accident, I mean so that I could reassure Ms. Butler." I, too, placed my hands in a prayer hand gesture. Two could play at the manipulation game.

For the first time since meeting Ms. Cramer, I could see a crack in the veneer. Color rose on her cheeks. She looked unsure and dropped her hands to her lap and then sat on them, as if steadying them.

Her voice got very soft, almost like Emily's when she's admitting to doing something naughty. "You see, I had fired Tina that very day." She looked down and wouldn't make eye contact. I felt sorry for Ms. Cramer in this moment. She was obviously wrestling with terrible guilt and was trying not to show it. "So, at the end of the day, she gathered her stuff and left. She usually took the bus or someone would give her ride. I guess she took the bus that day. She tripped on a root next to the curb and fell into the street. She was all alone. Someone hit her and just drove away."

"Have the police found the person driving the vehicle?" Ms. Cramer looked at me. She thought for a moment and shook her head. The question caught her off guard.

"So, it was a hit and run?" This was the first time I knew any details about what had happened to Tina.

"Uh, no, I'm sure it was just a terrible accident. I'm sure no one meant to hurt her, but they must have got scared or something. They probably just froze and ran away." She looked down at her nails and began picking under her fingernail. I sucked in my breath.

"Well, I certainly hope that whoever hit Tina would come forward—if it was just a terrible accident." I repeated her words. She examined her nails again, and then shook her head. "Yes, he should come forward, whoever was driving and hit her." She stopped looking at her nails and glanced around the sitting area.

"Thank you for listening, Denise. I don't know exactly what you did at your last position, but I know that you must have been pretty good at it." She smiled at me. This was the first genuine smile I had seen from her.

"Mostly talking, listening, praying and eating pizza." I raised my eyebrows at her and she laughed. She excused herself and walked away. I watched her as she left. She moved slowly and her shoulders sagged a bit and then all of a sudden, the façade returned and she marched off.

"Ms. Cramer?" I shouted down the hallway. She turned around at the mention of her name. "Ms. Butler also mentioned something about thefts?" She just shrugged and continued on her way.

After a quick trip to the bathroom, I hurried back to the activity room. The drawing class was ending and Alicia and I would need to once again escort the residents to their rooms and rearrange the activity room for book club. Lydia waved me over and showed me her progress on her bowl of fruit. I commented on her work as she handed me her bag and we made our way to her room. Her door was now closed.

She unlocked her door and walked in, directing me to place her bag on a table next to the window. "Oh hell, where's my watch?" I heard Lydia from the other room. I walked into her bedroom.

The bed was made and the room looked immaculate. Lydia rummaged around on her dresser. She turned to me: "Denise, use your young eyes and help me look for my watch. I'm sure that I left it here on the dresser, but I can't find it."

We both looked on the dresser. There was not much on the dresser, actually, only a lamp, a couple of books and a wooden box. I opened the box and looked at Lydia's jewelry, mostly costume pieces. I got down on the floor and looked under the dresser and looked behind the dresser and under the bed.

"Are you sure that you left it on the dresser?" I asked from the floor. I got up and walked into her small bathroom, looking at the items on the vanity and in the tiny garbage can.

"Yes, I took it off before class so it wouldn't get in the way. I cannot think where I might have put it. I was sure that I put it on the dresser." I thought back to the unlocked door earlier. Had she misplaced her watch or had someone stolen it?

I thought about my conversation with my sister over the weekend. During activities, the housekeeping staff cleaned. Could one of them have slipped in and taken the watch? That seemed the most logical. Today was beginning to look like there might indeed be a thief and/or a murderer at Riverview.

CHAPTER 19

I knocked on Ms. Cramer's door, unsure what I should do. I wasn't sure how she'd react to the news that I would deliver after our earlier conversation. I heard her say, "Come in." I opened the door and walked to the edge of her desk.

She looked up at me. "What can I do for you, Denise?" She gestured toward the uncomfortable folding chairs and I sat.

"I think that someone stole Lydia Shanks' watch while she was in drawing class this morning." I leaned forward, waiting for Ms. Cramer's response. She leaned back in her chair and thought for a moment.

"You mean, while we were talking earlier?" Ms. Cramer smiled "How strange! Are you sure that she didn't just lose it or misplace it?" Her response was almost automatic.

"I don't think so. I helped her look all over her bedroom. She said that she took it off before class and put it on her dresser. What should we do?" I waited for her response.

"I don't think that we can do anything, Denise. Ms. Shanks could have misplaced it. There's no reason to sound the alarms." Ms. Cramer rubbed her hands together. I could tell that she'd had this conversation before, and this was a perfectly practiced response. She straightened in her chair and with her expression I could feel the dismissal from her office.

As I stood up, I asked: "I understand what you're saying, but what if someone did take her watch? What would we do then?" I wondered if she would even speak.

"We take all complaints seriously here. Everyone who works at Riverview passed a police background check. Everyone who enters the building is recorded at our Reception desk." She gestured to the desk on the other side of the wall. "No one would steal at Riverview. That is impossible. Riverview has a reputation for honesty and security." She smiled again in her dismissal.

I pressed on, "Yes, but what if someone did?" I could tell now that she was tired of what she was considering an unacceptable line of questioning.

"Denise, there are older people here. They misplace things all the time. We cannot bother the police every single time some resident loses a necklace or watch or earrings..." She stopped abruptly when she realized that she had over spoke. Now I wondered how many watches, necklaces and jewelry *were* missing. She stood up and started to walk around her desk, presumably to escort me to the door.

"What would it hurt to call the police? Shouldn't we at least investigate?" Ms. Cramer turned her head to the side to examine me. I could tell that her patience had just come to an end.

"If you must know, we have cameras all over the place. If someone was stealing, we would see them. I review our videos daily. I have never witnessed anyone stealing at Riverview. It just doesn't happen here, especially under my watch, but I will look into it." Ms. Cramer motioned to the door, and I walked out. She shut the door behind me.

I stood there for a moment and determined that I'd find the security office and see if I could look at the tapes. I was not sure how I would do it, but I would.

CHAPTER 20

The security office was on the first floor, through the nursing unit. Most of Riverview was small apartments and suites, but once you went through the doors of the nursing unit, you entered a small hospital ward. Instead of pastel carpet and oak paneling, everything was antiseptic white. I wandered through the halls for about 15 minutes, looking and finally found the door with a small plastic nameplate: "Security." I knocked on the door. After what sounded like someone moving an elephant, the door swung open. One man was seated at the desk, looking at a computer screen. The other held the door for me.

I smiled at them as sweetly as I could. The room smelled like two day old baloney and coffee. The garbage can overflowed with Styrofoam cups and newspapers. The two men looked like Police Academy rejects. Both wore the standard Riverview polos with khaki pants, spotted with I what assumed were stains from a jelly sandwich. I felt like I was witnessing a true life cliché for security guards.

"Hello, my name is Denise. I help with the activities. I was wondering. I think that someone might have taken something from one of the residents. Would you be able to look at the monitors and check?" Once again, I smiled broadly. The man seated at the computer clicked something on his browser. He hadn't looked at me since I'd entered the room. I had a sick feeling it was not a cat video.

The two looked at each other. I could tell that they were irritated, but I wasn't sure if it was from my request or from the possibility of having to do any type of work. The other man sat down in the other chair in the room and scratched dangerously close to his nether regions. He rocked back and forth in his swivel chair. They remained silent, while the chair squeaked rhythmically, if not a little obscenely. I hoped it was unintentional. The man behind the screen finally looked up and almost opened his mouth, but then looked back at the screen.

Finally, the man at the computer grunted: "Only Ms. Cramer is allowed to see the monitor feed." He clicked on the mouse again. His eyes flicked to the screen. His eyes widened and his lips curved into an *O*. I wondered what he was looking at, but I thought it better to put that thought aside. Whatever it was, it was exciting. How I hoped he was watching cat videos!

"I understand. Of course, of course. I spoke with Ms. Cramer earlier. Perhaps you could look and tell me what you see?" I asked, hopeful. The man behind the computer looked shocked. Yep, the other guy was now scratching his nether regions with absolutely no regard for my discomfort. The squeaking increased. Yep, it was meant obscenely, but I was not sure how I would explain, "obscene chair squeaking" to the human resources representative. The two looked at each other.

The man behind the computer looked at the keyboard and bit his lip. Something was wrong, and he wasn't going to tell. Unless, of course, I used my mother super powers.

I have mother super powers. One is cooking the absolute best cheesy egg that my daughter loves. The other is what I call, "Wonder Woman's Lasso of Truth" face. Somehow the expression I make at that moment makes four-year-olds sing like a canary. I suspected that the same expression might work on a moron. At least I would try it. I made the expression and waited. I placed my hands on my hips, striking my best Wonder Woman pose.

"We didn't record anything this morning." Interesting.

The "Wonder Woman's Lasso of Truth" face is usually followed up with the repeating of whatever the four-year-old just said. It helps with clarification.

"You didn't record anything this morning?" I waited for his clarification. The cat video guy cleared his throat. The squeaky chair slowed.

"We accidently shut off the feed for about two hours." The ball scratcher practically growled at the man behind the computer. He emphasized "accidently." I wondered if I really wanted to know why they would have shut off the feed.

"Why or how did you shut off the feed?" The two then began to argue. I raised my palms and they grew silent.

"We never turned it on this morning, but I did just a few minutes ago," Cat Video Guy said brightly. So much for catching a thief on camera. I wondered how many times these guys might have not turned on the cameras. I shook my head.

I went to turn when Mr. Itchy Crotch asked: "Are you going to get us fired?" The squeaking stopped completely while he waited for my reply.

"I think you two can handle that on your own." I turned around and walked out. I was so frustrated at that point that I began my march to Louise's apartment. As I wandered through the hallways, I saw Dr. Martin.

"Hello, Denise. How are you today?" I could not believe the man actually remembered my name! His suit had a slight shininess to it, an iridescent navy blue. You couldn't take your eyes off it.

I stopped and shook his hand, "I'm fine, Dr. Martin. How are you?" The suit was transfixing or maybe it was the fact that it was so tight. I inwardly shook myself. I needed to speak with Louise.

"I'm doing well. How is your delightful mother? Did I tell you that she helped me find my house a few years ago?" he asked eagerly. I was sure he was about to tell me about his ex-wife again.

Before he could go on, I answered, "She's doing really well. She loves retirement." I began to walk away when he went on.

"Retirement must be great. I wish I could do that, if not for the ex. Never satisfied, that one. Just wants to extract her pound of flesh, if you know what I mean." He flashed his radiant smile, but the joke was lame.

"Yes?" I replied. How did this man want me to respond? He really needed to speak to a therapist about his ex-wife. He might be a silver fox, but he was bitter. His face became somber.

"I noticed that you were speaking with security a little while ago. Is everything okay?" I was staring once again at his mesmerizing suit, and my eyes shot up. Maybe security didn't have their eyes on much, but Dr. Martin certainly knew what was going on.

"How did you know?" I asked before I could stop myself.

"Riverview is very important to me. I pay attention to everything," he spoke seriously. He continued, "Of course, that's probably why my ex-wife left." He waited for my laughter, but again I couldn't muster even the most tepid tee-hee. I debated whether I should say anything about the theft.

"I think that someone took Ms. Shanks' watch from her room, but security doesn't have anything on tape." I hope that I hadn't just tossed the two guards under the bus, but perhaps someone should not have been looking at cat videos. I could tell that Dr. Martin considered what I said. He leaned his head back.

"I see. Did Mrs. Shanks tell Ms. Cramer about her watch?" He listened intently for my reply.

"No, she didn't say anything to her," I answered. Mrs. Shanks had just shrugged and mumbled something about getting old. I'd hated the defeat that I'd witnessed in her response. "But I told Ms. Cramer," I offered.

"You brought this to Ms. Cramer's attention?" he asked with no emotion. He was cold. "It sounds like she might have just misplaced the item." Lord have mercy! Was there a section in the employee handbook with catch phrases that all employees should use in case of theft?

"I don't think that she misplaced it, sir. I was there when she took it off before class and I was there with her afterwards to look for it." He considered what I was saying.

"Well, then; if you brought it to Ms. Cramer's attention, it will be taken care of." With that, he began to walk away, but he stopped. "Denise?"

"Yes, sir?" I waited to hear what he would say.

"Let's keep this between us, for now." I went to speak but closed my mouth. He walked away. I continued on my way to Louise's suite, but I felt so frustrated.

By the time I arrived at her door, I was about to explode. I tapped insistently and waited. I knocked louder, and finally Louise swung open the door. "I was in the bathroom, if you don't mind."

Her expression transformed from indignant to embarrassed. "Oh, it's you, Denise. What can I do for you?" She stood in the doorway and tapped her foot.

"Are you busy?" Louise raised her eyebrows and hooked her thumb over her shoulder pointing to the bathroom. "Oh, I see. I wanted to tell you that someone took Lydia Shanks' watch." I whispered the last part.

Louise leaned against the door jam. "That's important. Did you report it?" I nodded. "What did Cramer say?" she snarled.

"She would look into it, I guess. I went to security to see if they had anyone on tape in that area during that time, and they'd forgotten to turn the cameras on." I huffed and put my hands on my hips. Louise smiled at my pose like I smile at Emily when she poses. "What?"

"You look just like your mother did when she was trying to argue about her grades. We just need to get some proof." Louise shifted uncomfortably. She gazed at the wall behind me.

"What do you suggest? I haven't noticed any stolen jewels just lying around, have you?" I asked sarcastically. Louise shifted again and looked over my shoulder again.

"Denise, that would be great if you could do that for me, but I really need to get back to the toilet." She announced and abruptly closed her door. *What was that about?* I wondered.

I turned around and ran smack into Jason. I immediately blushed. How could he have not heard Louise's bathroom announcement?

"Hello," I said awkwardly. He smiled smugly. Yep, he'd heard what she'd said and he thought it was funny. I guess it was a little funny.

I thought back to our conversation on Friday evening. I looked at my shoes. I remembered what I'd implied about his physique, his extremely hot physique. At least, I didn't say it directly and it wasn't at work. Who wants a sexual harassment suit on her hands?

"Why did you go to the security department?" His smug expression was replaced with intensity. I moved to step around him, but he moved, blocking my escape.

"How did you…" I stopped. I guess there was no need for working cameras in this place because everyone already knew what was going on. "Is this really any of your business?" His expression changed from intense to seriously annoyed. I ducked quickly to his left and moved around him. He reached out and tapped my shoulder. I turned toward him and I could tell it was taking everything in him to keep from grabbing and shaking me.

"Denise, you are messing around with something dangerous, and you need to stop it." He grabbed my upper arms. His hold was tight, but not squeezing, yet. I began to protest, and he immediately released me from his grip. "I'm sorry I grabbed you." He dropped his hands at his side and looked ashamed.

I rubbed my arms, even though they didn't hurt. I was shocked and a little shaken. What was going on?

"Did you really report a theft to Ms. Cramer?" I looked down at the carpet, trying to decide which shade of pink it was. I didn't want to answer his question. I decided to redirect.

"Jason, why don't you tell me what you're up to?" He looked at me. I could tell that he was trying to weigh whether or not he should tell me the truth. He sighed.

"I can't, right now." I knew he wouldn't tell me what was going on with him. I was about to speak, but he continued, "You need to stop poking your nose in this or something is going happen to you. You have no idea what you're doing here." I shook my head.

"Then why would I tell you what I'm up to? Why do you care what I'm doing?" I waited to hear his response. He was blank. I walked away. He just stood there in the hallway, or I like to think that he might have.

CHAPTER 21

I took the elevator to the lobby. I was at the end of my shift, anyway, so I headed to the employee locker room and retrieved my purse from my locker. I felt so frustrated after my earlier interactions. Everyone seemed to want to ignore the fact that someone was stealing at Riverview. Was it a conspiracy or laziness? I slammed my locker shut and flung my purse over my shoulder.

"That was loud," a voice startled me. I swung around to the voice. I was face to face with pimple face. He was standing a little too close for comfort. I stepped back and stepped on someone's foot.

I turned around to find one of the other aides. I remembered him sitting down with Jason and me in the break room on my first day. Perhaps I now had an idea who might have been stealing at Riverview and maybe even who'd killed Tina Moore.

"I'm so sorry. I didn't see you there." I smiled so hard that my face hurt. I straightened myself up and looked back and forth between the two men. "Well, I'm at the end of my shift. What about you two?" I attempted to sound casual.

"Nah, we ain't done," the aide spoke. Somehow he looked about ten feet tall and three feet thick. I smiled again. You can never beat smiling. Smile when your heart is breaking, smile when you fear for your life... The two seethed at me. I kept smiling.

"Well, if you gentlemen would excuse me, I'm heading home. See you tomorrow!" I made a move toward the door, but neither man would move. I stepped toward one or the other, but neither moved. "Is there are problem?" I asked innocently.

"You tell me," pimple face said. He stepped closer to me. For a skinny punk, he was really threatening. I realized at this moment that I needed to use my brain because something bad was about to happen to me. I remembered my purse on my shoulder. Today I was carrying my jumbo purse because Emily had used my Coach purse to carry her crayons and she'd left it outside—in the heat.

I shifted the bag. I suppose that I could have tried to hit them with the bag, but I was positive that he or the brick wall would probably snatch it before I could swing it. I thought about what I might be carrying: lipstick, brush, wallet, cellphone, 20 pens, some devotional book and lots of fast food restaurant napkins. Why did I forget to pack a gun today? Oh wait, I never packed heat.

I reached into my bag and yanked out the devotional book. I held it up and looked at the two men. In that moment, I decided to use one of my most powerful repelling powers, the one thing sure to shut down any conversation and drive someone away from you faster than a speeding bullet: poorly executed evangelism.

"Have you ever read this book?" I looked at the two men with what I am sure was a crazed look in my eyes. The two men looked at each other. "I can tell from your expression that you're not familiar with the works of Anthony De Mello. So good. He interprets the Gospel in such new and beautiful ways. You're familiar with the Gospel?" I looked at both of them and took a step closer. "You know Jesus?" I asked. The Brick Wall was completely puzzled with my questions and Pimple Face looked like he might explode. I pushed on. "Where do you guys go to church? I hope you don't mind me asking, but I want to know what I can do today to ensure that you two will go to church this Sunday at St. Christopher's Church. I tell you that Rev. Foucher preaches an inspired word and let me tell you about the body and the blood." I started rattling on with such an evangelical fervor that my father was probably rolling in his Episcopal grave. I hoped that this was having the right effect.

I stepped closer to the two men. If they could be threatening, I could as well. They might be able to hurt me physically, but I could definitely drive someone away by talking too much, at least that's what my ex-husband had said.

The two men stepped back. Their expressions turned from intimidating to perplexed to utterly confused. It was working. I went in for the kill, "So, who wants to come to church this Sunday? I know we could all use a little Jesus, am I right?" I plastered the most bizarre smile I could conjure on my face. I should have been nominated for an Academy Award for scene chewing.

"Uh, I'll think about it." The larger man scratched his arm and looked down. He chewed on his lower lip and turned to leave. I turned my maniacal expression on pimple face. He looked after his brick wall friend and followed him out, scowling.

"Don't think too hard about it! Have faith! We could all ride together!" I almost shouted the last part as the two men exited. I released a huge sigh.

"That was probably the funniest performance I've ever seen." I turned to see Jason standing across the room. How long had he been there? He leaned against the wall with his arms crossed.

"I don't know what you mean. I love Anthony de Mello and they *should* go to St. Christopher's. I won't be there, but *they* should definitely go." I held my crazed expression and then barked out a laugh. We both laughed. I felt tears start to well up in my eyes. I wiped them with the back of my hand. "How long were you standing there? I thought I was going to have to start shouting for help."

"Long enough to know that you could handle them, for now. Why don't I walk you to your car?" He extended an arm to me. I looped my arm through his. I leaned against him and welcomed the warmth.

"That would be really nice," I squeaked before the tears rolled down my face. He led me down the hallway and through a side entrance to the parking lot. When we were outside, I could feel the warmth on my skin and my nerves felt less frayed. My two bullies were nowhere to be seen so I attempted to pull away my arm, but he held my arm tightly until we arrived at the door of my car. I looked up at him to say thank you, but for a moment I lost my breath. He looked down at me and leaned ever so slightly forward. I thought he might be going in for a kiss. Instead, he brushed a piece of lint from shoulder.

"Thanks, Jason." I opened my car door and got in. He shut the door behind me and tapped twice on the door. I waved at him and then I watched as he returned to the building.

CHAPTER 22

When I arrived home, I immediately locked the door and attempted to drive thoughts of the encounter with pimple face and the brick wall from my head. I took a shower. I walked to the coffee shop, but promptly walked home when I remembered that I saw pimple face across the street on the previous weekend. I tried reading my book until I picked up Emily, but I could only read a few paragraphs at a time.

I got in my car and headed to the grocery store on Tchoupitoulus. I moved quickly through the aisle, looking over my shoulder as I went. I felt sure I would see the two toughs.

While I pushed my cart through the doors into the parking lot, I scanned the street. All I observed were shoppers picking up groceries. I rushed to my car and popped the trunk. I tossed my groceries in, probably crushing my tomatoes, and I hopped into the front seat. I slammed the door and clicked the lock.

I attempted to pull out of the parking lot onto Tchoupitoulus. I wanted to turn left, but the traffic was heavy, so I turned right. I would just have to turn around in a block or two. As I drove, I looked at the businesses along the route. Over the last few years in New Orleans, a lot of gentrification had occurred. Little gyms had popped up along the street between auto supply shops and a bar. I drove a little further until my eyes fell on one store, a hold-over from a rougher time on the street—a pawn shop.

I pulled the car over and parked. I knew that it might be a longshot, but what if someone had taken the stolen items from Riverview and hocked them here. I already had an idea that my suspect lived in the neighborhood, so why would he go very far to sell his ill-gotten gains?

I crossed the street and pushed the buzzer at the shop door. I waited for another buzz to pull the door and walk in. The business was crammed full of stereos, televisions, weed whackers, and any electronic device one could imagine. I made my way to the display cases. They, too, were overstuffed with small jewelry boxes and small firearms.

I studied the case, but I wasn't sure what I should look for. I had no idea what to look for. When I'd talked with the residents a few weeks ago, I'd never asked them to describe their missing items. At the same time, there was so much in the case that unless I knew what to look for, my expedition would take weeks.

"Help you find something, honey?" A surprisingly kind voice growled from the grizzled old man behind the counter.

"Uh, I'm not sure, yet." I scanned the case again. I remembered Louise's description of her friend's pendant. It seemed unlikely, but if I could find this piece of jewelry, I might have the proof I needed to speak to the police.

"Do you have any Wedgewood?" As soon as I asked, I knew I'd made a mistake. He had no idea what I was talking about.

"Baby, I don't know the names of the stuff, but we got a lot of jewelry. I just buy it and I sell it." He answered regretfully.

I decided to go another direction. "I think that my friend might have brought a piece of jewelry down here that he was getting rid of. It was his grandmother's. It would be blue with white on it, maybe set in gold, a pendant on a chain. I really wanted it, but I didn't tell him in time." I smiled and continued, "He kind of has acne."

I waited for a reply. The old man squinted at me. "I don't buy stolen property." Strange that he would realize that it was probably stolen from my story. He could tell that I wasn't being completely honest. Heck, he probably thought I was some jerk who liked to buy stolen property.

"Of course, you don't, sir. Did you see that pendant?" I asked before he kicked me out of his store. He scratched his cheek. The moment felt like an eternity while he decided whether or not to answer me.

"Was it an antique?" He tapped his lips with a finger and turned around for a moment. He pawed through a stack of business cards and found the one. He handed the card to me.

"When people come by with antiques, I send them there. You looking for anything else?" I read the card, not recognizing the name, but I knew the address. The place was only a few blocks from my house on Magazine Street. I thanked the man and immediately hopped into my car. I only had a few minutes before 4 and many antique stores closed by 4.

I made my way to Magazine Street, avoiding potholes and bumper to bumper traffic. I circled the block twice looking for parking near the store and gave up. I opted to park on Chestnut and walk. I rushed to the tiny antique shop. The owner was just walking toward the front window in what I can only assume was a move to close the door.

I pushed the door open and marched right in. The owner in his red sweater vest and bow tie frowned. He walked towards me. "Madame, I'm about to close. It's almost 4."

"Yes, of course, sir; but perhaps you could help me find something for my great aunt. She's looking for something Wedgewood." I knew as soon as I dropped a name, he would drop the attitude. His eyebrows rose behind his tiny round glasses. He stopped and pivoted to the case on his left and motioned.

I followed him and scanned the display case. I could not believe the contrast between this store and the pawn shop. For a tiny space, he made it seem almost empty and yet there must have been about 50 items in the case. Vases, small ash trays, boxes from the traditional Wedgewood blue to lavender and black filled the case, but I didn't see any pendants.

"Do you have any pendants?" Again he raised his eyebrows. The man walked to a case on the opposite wall filled with jewelry. Some was costume, some most definitely was real.

"You will have to be a little more specific."

"A Wedgewood pendant, blue and white, set in gold?" With my description, he pulled a key ring from his pocket to open the case. He stepped behind the counter and bent down and mumbled. He rummaged for something near the cash register.

"What?" I asked.

He turned around, having found his key to the display case. He opened the back of the case and reached around. "I said, you're in luck. Someone just brought in a piece like that." He was getting excited. He immediately produced a little box and opened it. Lying on the black velvet was a gold heart, about two inches wide, with a little piece of Wedgwood. The image was a Greco-Roman styled man and woman.

"Do you get a lot of pieces like this?" Could this be the necklace or were there thousands of these?

"Every now and then, but not often. People don't usually want to wear Wedgwood, you know." He wrinkled his nose like the idea was truly distasteful.

"Where did this one come from? Someone's estate, I imagine?" Oh please tell me pimple face sold this to you, please, please...

"Actually, a woman brought this by about two weeks ago. Her aunt had left it to her, but she just didn't care for it." He picked up the pendant and chain, and gently placed the piece in my hand. I turned it over and looked at the price tag, $75. "It's on sale this week."

"Do you know what her name was? The lady who brought in the necklace?" I tried to sound casual, but my excitement was growing. He pulled off his glasses and wiped them on a handkerchief. I wasn't sure if he would reply.

"Nelson, I think." I didn't know anyone named Nelson. Looked like a dead end here. He pushed his glasses back on his nose and began to reach for a receipt book. "Are you interested in the necklace?" he asked impatiently.

I certainly did not want to buy it, but I needed Louise to see it. Would the item be there tomorrow? Probably, but I couldn't be sure.

"May I take a picture of it? To be sure this is the one she wants?" Again he showed such distaste as he placed the pendant back in the box, but he didn't close it. I pulled out my cellphone and snapped a picture. He shut the box and promptly huffed while he returned it to the display case.

"It's 4 o'clock. I need to close, Madame." The man dismissed me and I thanked him. With glee, I held my phone tightly and ran to my car. I sent a text with the picture to Louise. I needed to speak with Louise, but first I'd have to pick up my daughter.

While I drove, my phone rang and I immediately picked it, hoping it was Louise. At first, I didn't recognize the voice on the other end. It definitely was not Louise.

"Hello, Denise; it's Jason. I was calling to check on you after your incident this morning." I felt my face warm. I was so glad he couldn't see me right now.

"Oh, yes, hi! I'm doing okay. I was just about to pick up my daughter." He actually called me. I was curious. I was thrilled. I was tongue-tied. "How are you?"

"I'm okay." The phone went silent for a moment. I almost thought that the call had dropped when he spoke again. "I think that we should talk."

"Okay, sure, when?" I arrived at Emily's preschool and parked the car. Parents and children milled about on the street. I glanced at my watch. I would be late picking up Emily, if I didn't get off the phone.

"Can you meet now?" He was impatient.

"No, I'm picking up my daughter. Is there another time?" I didn't want to blow him off, but after school care would charge by the minute.

"Are you going to the park this afternoon? I could meet you all there. I really need to talk to you." His voice was persuasive. Obviously, he really needed something from me, not perhaps what I wanted him to need from me.

"Sure, we'll be there in about 15 minutes."

CHAPTER 23

When Emily and I arrived at the playground at the park, I opened the visor mirror and examined my face. Any traces of mascara were gone. I ran my fingers through my hair. I dug through my purse looking for some lipstick, but all I could find was an old chap stick. Emily kicked my seat in protest.

"Okay, okay," I said, and with that, she launched herself from the car at breakneck speed. I may not be able to do a lot of things right, but according to Emily, I was the best mommy in the world (at least for this afternoon). I sat on the bench while she headed for a swing.

She pumped her legs and quickly was almost horizontal to the ground. I shouted my warning from my perch, checking my phone. Again, I looked in my purse. Didn't I have a comb, at least? I felt strong hands on my shoulders and almost craned my neck jerking to look at Jason. He stood behind me on the bench.

"You scared me!" I exclaimed. He shrugged and walked around the bench, sitting next to me. I placed a hand over my heart, trying to steady my breath.

"Sorry." He stretched his legs out and draped his arms over the back of the bench. I was suddenly sitting on the edge of the bench. How was it possible that one man could take up that much space so quickly?

"Thanks for meeting with me, Denise. I needed to talk with you." He turned his head and examined me. "Why are you sitting all the way on the end? You look like you're going to fall off the bench." He sat up slightly and I scooted a little closer. I would have loved to scoot even closer, but oh well.

"What do you need to talk to me about?" He looked at Emily swinging and he smiled. I admired his profile. I noticed a little bump to his nose, probably broken at one point. He wore jeans and a sweatshirt.

"How old is your daughter?" He watched her swing.

"She's four," I answered. I watched her as well. She giggled at some mysterious joke.

"Is she your only one?" He looked back at me. I nodded. "She's cute. She's got your cheeks. Where's her dad?"

"I adopted her after I got divorced," I answered. His smiled broadened even more. I would have liked to talk about Emily all day, but I wanted to know what he wanted. "What did you want to talk about?"

"I need to know why you went to the security office today, but I really want to know what you're doing at Riverview." He was serious. He stared into my eyes. I wanted to look away, but his eyes were so beautiful. I was sure that he could read my mind at that moment. I blushed.

"I went to the security office to see if I could see who might have gone into Lydia Shanks' suite and took her watch while we were in class. After my encounter with pimple face and his sidekick, I think that I have an idea, but I don't have any proof." I felt relief telling someone else about the investigation. I had worried that perhaps Jason was involved, but in my gut, I knew he wasn't.

He shook his head. He smiled. "Pimple face and side-kick? That's a good description for those clowns." We both laughed a little. His laugh was throaty and his eyes crinkled at the side when he laughed. He asked again, "So, what are you doing at Riverview?"

"I'm helping Louise find proof that someone is stealing at Riverview and that someone killed Tina Moore." I spoke the words softly and quickly. I looked at my lap. I wasn't sure that I wanted to see his expression. I continued, "I think that I might have found something."

I showed him the picture on my phone. He glanced at it. He was silent for a while.

"What is that?" he asked. He pressed the screen to enlarge the picture.

"I think that this was a pendant that belonged to one of the residents, a friend of Ms. Butler's. A woman sold this to the antique store, claiming it was her grandmother's, but I'm almost positive this was stolen from Ms. Lee." He looked unconvinced, but he asked me for the name of the store.

"I'm glad that you told me." He paused, "I think that you need to stop now." Again, he stared into my eyes, like he was attempting to hypnotize me.

"I know," I said. I thought he might be right, but I still needed Louise's confirmation before I went to the police with what I had. I looked back at the picture on my phone. Still no text from Louise, nor a call.

Emily jumped off her swing and ran to the bench. She marched right up to Jason and asked: "Would you swing me around?"

"Excuse me?" Jason stood up and looked down at Emily. She placed her hands on her hips and looked back at him. "Don't you want to know what my name is first?" he asked, but she just giggled. I swear that the man had that effect on every woman, no matter what age.

"What's your name?" she shyly asked.

"Jason," he answered. She extended her right hand forward to shake his hand. I was so proud. He actually giggled when she took his hand.

"Swing me around!" Emily demanded now that she knew his name. He shook his head and looked to check with me. He then picked her up and swung her around once, placing her carefully on her feet. He started to move like he was leaving.

"Where are you going?" Emily asked him. She took hold of his hand and swung it back and forth. He looked down at her.

"I was going to dinner," he answered her, swinging her hand gently.

"Can I go with you?" Emily asked. I immediately apologized and tried to explain to Emily that Jason probably wanted to eat by himself or with his family. I looked over to see if he was nodding in agreement. He probably had a date with a Victoria Secret underwear model.

Jason interrupted me, "Of course, y'all could come to dinner with me. I'm just going to Camellia Grill, if you want to come." He offered genuinely. Before I could refuse, Emily shouted, "Yes!"

Emily immediately began to pull Jason towards the parked cars. She also took my hand and walked between Jason and me. We walked to our cars and headed to dinner at Camellia Grill. At dinner, we sat at the counter and ate our burgers, fries and milk shakes. Emily delighted in snatching fries from Jason's plate, while he pretended to look away. Most of our conversation revolved around Emily and all her favorite things. Jason told stories about his two nieces and nephew who was just about Emily's age. Our dinner felt like a family dinner and yet I still knew so little about him.

After dinner, Jason paid the check and kissed Emily on the top of her head, "Girls, I've had a wonderful evening with you two, but I need to go." He hugged Emily. "I really liked meeting you, Emily." I wondered if he ever babysat because this guy was a natural with kids. He placed a hand on my shoulder. "This was nice. Good night, Denise." He walked out the restaurant while Emily and I finished our shakes. Emily and I waved as he walked away.

It only occurred to me as I watched his firm bottom leave that I'd forgotten to ask what *he* was doing at Riverview, but something told me it was more than being a CNA. He was looking for answers at Riverview and perhaps answers to the very questions I had.

CHAPTER 24

That evening, after I tucked Emily in bed, I curled up on the couch and turned on the television. I flipped through the channels, trying to find something reassuring and non-violent. I finally settled on *Golden Girls*, but then I remembered what I thought about Lydia Shanks. Then I'd think about Riverview and then I'd think about pimple face and his mammoth friend. Despite the success of my discovery of the pendant and my unexpected dinner with Jason, I felt edgy.

I needed to speak with Louise. I wanted her confirmation as to whether or not this was the pendant, and if so, what next? I would have to find a way to avoid those goons until I could alert the police. *Maybe I should call the police right now,* I thought, but I didn't really have enough proof. I looked at my cellphone.

It had been hours, and I'd heard nothing from Louise. I was sure she'd have to have seen the picture by now. I waited until I could stand it no more. I called Louise.

The phone rang and Louise picked up. "Hello?" Her voice was sing-songy. I looked at my watch and groaned. I must have caught her at dinner.

"Hello, Louise; it's Denise. Did you get my text earlier?" I waited while she spoke to someone who must have been sitting with her at dinner. She laughed and shushed her companion. Was she flirting with someone?

"No, I haven't had my phone with me all day. I went with my niece Barbara to Canal Place this afternoon and we actually went to the movies. Such fun. I need to introduce you two. I know you'd get along great." I listened as Louise prattled on.

"Louise, please take a look at the picture. I think it might be the necklace you told me about." I waited as she put down her phone, presumably to fiddle with the screen and put on her glasses. I could hear more fumbling and then she must have put the phone back to her ear. She laughed again with her dining companion.

"Where did you find it?" All mirth left Louise's voice, "Wait. I can't really hear in here. We need to meet. Come over tomorrow." She hung up.

CHAPTER 25

The next morning I dropped Emily off almost 30 minutes early at school. I decided that I was going to the police with what I had so far. Something was going on at Riverview and it was a police matter. I knew my limitations.

I arrived at the station on Magazine Street and spoke briefly with someone at the front counter. At this time in the morning, the station was busy. Some officers were coming off a shift and other were starting. The officer at the front counter directed me to sit in one of the wooden chairs in the hallway in front of the desk, as he made a few calls.

I looked down at my watch. I still had about an hour before my five hour shift at Riverview began. I looked at the officer behind the counter. He avoided my gaze. They were busy today.

After twenty minutes, another officer approached me. She was a heavy-set woman with smooth olive skin and the clearest and kindest brown eyes I've ever seen. Her expression was apologetic.

"Ma'am, I'm so sorry that you had to wait. I'm Officer Perez. Officer Donner said that you had information about a crime?" She settled into the chair next to me and pulled out a small notebook from her front chest pocket. The hallway was noisy and just getting noisier.

"I'm sorry to do this here, but our conference room and meeting rooms are being used right at the moment. This has been a busy morning." As if on cue, three men burst through the front doors and barreled down the hall. One man was in handcuffs between two officers. The man in handcuffs shouted and swore, obviously drunk or high, his t-shirt torn and covered in mud.

"You got mud on my shirt. This is my favorite t-shirt, you sons of bi..." The man momentarily caught my eye and leered, correcting himself, "you sons of beaches. How are you, little mama?" He winked at me as he said it. The officers yanked him down the hallway and he let out a yelp.

We both watched the man and then exchanged glances. "You looking for a boyfriend?" she asked as she gestured with her thumb in the prisoner's direction. I vigorously shook my head. We both laughed.

She cleared her throat. "Like I was saying, we've been a little busy. Please tell me what brings you here today." She poised her pen to begin to write.

I drew a deep breath and began, "I'm working at Riverview and I think that someone there is stealing from the residents and might be involved in the death of another employee." I blurted it out and pulled out my cellphone. I produced the picture of the Wedgewood necklace and showed it to the woman. I noticed that she stopped taking notes.

She scrunched her face like she was trying to understand every word I said, but I was speaking in Mandarin Chinese, "Why don't you slow down and start again? What's your name?" I gave her my name and address.

Bit by bit, I told her my story. I started by telling her about going to the worship service at Riverview and meeting Louise. I repeated the story Louise had told me about the pendant, and that Tina Moore looked for it and couldn't find it. I also expressed my own doubts, at the time, but that after I became friends with Louise that I agreed to investigate the thefts and possible murder. At that, she stopped me.

"Wait, you took a job to investigate whether or not someone was stealing at Riverview and whether or not that person and or persons might have killed a woman?" I could tell by her tone that she didn't approve. She closed her notebook and placed it in her lap. She turned her whole body so that she could look at me. "Ms. Reed, you seem like a fairly reasonable and smart person, but what you did is really stupid, not to mention dangerous. Why did you do that?"

I nodded my head in agreement with Officer Perez. "You're right. I know it was foolish." I didn't really think that much about why I took the job. Sure, I was trying to help Louise investigate thefts and murder. Sure, I needed something to do, but I knew that these were not the reasons I'd entered this investigation. I thought back to Tina Moore's obituary. I realized that I saw a little of myself in Tina Moore. Like me, she was a single mother who just wanted to help people. Both of us had been dumped from our positions, but where I had just hidden at home, feeling sorry for myself, Tina Moore was dead.

Officer Perez waited for me to say more, but I stayed silent. I wasn't sure how to explain my relationship to a dead woman, a person I never met. I suddenly felt tearful, but I didn't cry. Officer Perez picked up her notebook.

"What happened wasn't right," I finally answered. Officer Perez nodded her head in agreement and asked me to continue my story.

I told her that after I got a job at Riverview that I spoke with a few residents about their missing items. In fact, just the other day someone else had an item go missing. I then told her about finding the necklace at the antique store and I proudly produced the phone.

She pulled some glasses from her pocket and put them on to look at the pendant. "That's lovely, but how do you know this is the same necklace?" I told her about sending the picture to Louise. She shook her head thoughtfully.

"Ms. Reed, someone may very well be stealing at Riverview, but if the residents haven't reported these thefts, there isn't much hope of figuring out who's doing this," she said ruefully. She tapped her pen against her notebook.

"But, Officer, I think I know who's behind it. He's in housekeeping over there. He kind of threatened me yesterday." I pleaded with her. Her face filled with disgust.

"What's his name?" I realized one glaring error in my meticulous reporting. I only called Alicia's boyfriend "pimple face." I had no idea what his name was.

"I don't know his name, yet. He dates my supervisor, Alicia Jones," I offered. I knew that my story sounded a little far-fetched. Officer Perez looked at me with such sincerity. I knew that she was trying to deliver bad news as graciously as she could.

"I will make a report and turn this over to our theft division. It will open a file and if you can get the residents to make a report or if Riverview would make a report, we will already have your information to work with." Her offer was pretty good, but...

"Will you investigate over there?" I asked. Her chin dropped as she considered what she would say. She looked weary.

"That's up to the theft division." I hung my head, but she continued, "but they might pursue this, especially with what you've brought to us. No officer wants to hear about someone ripping off old ladies. I tell you what, I'll write this up right now and put it on the division chief's desk. That way, he'll see it first thing when he comes in." She checked her watch and nodded her head. "He's due in around noon today, but he may call in for messages. At the very least, I know that Officer Stone will start asking some questions, maybe even this afternoon." She offered reassurance and hope.

"What about Tina Moore's accident?" I asked. She flushed slightly.

"That's an ongoing investigation," she answered in monotone.

She once again checked with me about the spelling of my name, address and cellphone number. She had me text her phone with the picture that she would print out in her report. I guess it was a start, and I felt that maybe the police would pursue the matter.

I looked down at my watch. I had about 20 minutes to get to Riverview. I could probably get there in ten and run to Louise's apartment and tell her about the developments in the investigation.

"Here's my card, Ms. Reed. If you think of anything else, please feel free to call me. I put my cell on the back. You need to be careful." She held out her business card to me as she rose from her seat. I thanked her and took the card.

I actually arrived at Riverview in eight minutes. I felt so excited to tell Louise about what I'd done. The police had my statement and what proof I could produce. Somehow I trusted that Officer Perez would not let me down.

When I walked into the building, I didn't take the elevator. I actually ran up the stairs to Louise's door. When I reached her door, I was wheezing. I hadn't run like that since high school, and I never ran in high school if I could help it. I caught my breath and pounded on her door. I heard nothing from the other side of the door. I waited and knocked again.

I decided that she might have gone to the dining room for breakfast. I jogged down the hall, moving around walkers and canes like a motorcycle in rush hour traffic. When I arrived at the dining room, I surveyed the room, but I didn't see Louise.

I noticed Toots in a corner and I went to him. "Toots, have you seen Miss Louise this morning?" Toots looked up from his oatmeal. He scrunched his face a moment. He finished chewing his oatmeal. I swear he must chew twenty times on each bite.

Finally, after wiping his lips with his cloth napkin, he spoke: "I saw her last night, for a little bit. We were supposed to have a drink after dinner, but she disappeared." I could hear the disappointment in his voice. He returned the napkin to his lap and took another bite of oatmeal.

"Did you have dinner with her last night?" He continued to chew. I waited while he once again lifted the napkin to wipe his mouth. He shook his head. He looked disgusted.

"She sat with Dr. Martin. Those two were laughing and carrying on." Toots was painting a picture of Louise and Dr. Martin flirting. The image of them in a romantic embrace was now burned in my head, but I doubted the actual encounter was as sordid as Toots made it sound. Where was Louise? I had news and I was exploding to tell her.

I left the dining room and returned to the lobby to sign-in. I entered the elevator and as the door was closing, I glimpsed the brick wall pushing a vacuum in the lobby. I pressed the door close button. I hoped he hadn't seen me. The doors shut at last.

When the doors opened, I headed for the activity room and looked at the schedule posted on the wall. This morning's activity was Tai Chi. Alicia came in whistling. I waved at her. She gave a tight smile and started moving chairs.

We made quick work of the room, moving the chairs and pushing back tables for Tai Chi. Alicia handed me the names of half of the participants of this class and she took the other half and we went to escort our residents. Before we could leave the room, Ms. Cramer stepped into the room.

"Alicia, Denise, I'm so glad I caught you before your day started." She waved us toward her. I crossed the room and smiled at Ms. Cramer. This morning she sported a beige pant suit, cream-colored blouse and paisley scarf. The woman had some style.

Alicia moved nervously and shifted back and forth while we waited to hear what Ms. Cramer had to say. Alicia looked a little more hyper this morning. Her usual smooth ponytail was frazzled and her pink smock actually had a smudge. I tried to pay attention to what Ms. Cramer was saying, but my mind kept returning to Louise. Where was she?

"Do you understand?" I tuned back into what Ms. Cramer had said right at that question. I had completely blanked and she must have known it. She huffed and said, "I said, when you go to escort a resident, our new regulations state that you should have someone else with you. Okay?" She awaited my reply.

I nodded and Alicia nodded. Alicia scratched and pulled at her collar under her smock. As she adjusted her smock, my eye caught the silver gleam of a broach pined to her shirt just below the collar. It was iridescent white, like pearls.

"What's that?" I innocently asked Alicia, pointing at the broach. She adjusted her smock again to cover the broach, but I was sure I knew what I saw. I had seen the broach before, a cluster of freshwater pearls set in silver. Ms. Cramer looked as well.

"It's nothing. It was a gift to me from someone special." A dreamy expression washed over her face. Alicia placed her hand over the broach, but Ms. Cramer reached out toward Alicia's hand. Alicia moved her hand and opened her smock slightly so we could both admire the pin—Louise's pin. I wondered if Ms. Cramer recognized the item, but as usual I couldn't tell what she was thinking.

"That's just lovely, Alicia. You say that you got that from someone special? That sounds pretty romantic. What a beautiful gift." With that, Ms. Cramer smiled and marched away. Alicia covered the broach again. I was shocked. Alicia had Louise's broach. How did she have Louise's broach?

"Wow! That sure is beautiful, Alicia. It reminds me of something." I tried to sound enthusiastic, but instead I was filling with dread. Alicia smiled at me and I could see satisfaction in her eyes, like she'd finally gotten something that she really wanted. I felt disgusted. We both stood in the empty room and it felt like the area filled with silence, despite the movement of residents entering.

"Have you seen Ms. Butler this morning, Alicia?" I asked her unsteadily. A shadow crossed over her face for a brief moment like she was deeply considering my question.

"Haven't seen her yet today," she answered in an overly cheerful tone. I hadn't known Alicia long, so I wasn't sure if she was lying to me. She headed out the door and scurried down the hallway to get her residents. I would have followed her, but the brick wall and pimple face stepped into hallway behind her, both escorting a resident to the activity room. I turned in the opposite direction and sped toward my first resident, Mr. O'Keefe on the third floor. I hoped they hadn't seen me.

I looked over my shoulder and my gaze locked on the two thugs. They definitely saw me. Now the question would be: could I avoid them long enough to speak with Louise and get out of Riverview without having my clock cleaned?

I continued to the third floor. I kept looking behind me, scanning to make sure that I wasn't alone. I didn't want to run into them again. I wondered if I should just leave and try to find help, but if I left before the end of my shift, I could be fired. I also still needed to find Louise.

I called her cellphone at least six times that morning, while escorting residents to different activities. Every time I saw Alicia, I wanted to shake her. I wanted to know how she got Louise's broach, and I wanted to know what she'd done to Louise. Had something happened to Louise?

I was about to call Louise once more, right before the next activity, when I saw Jason. I realized that I needed some help, if I was going to find Louise. I was close to freaking out. I waved at him.

"What's up?" I pulled him aside, while the others passed us in the hallway.

"I think something has happened to Louise Butler," I hissed the last part out. Jason was blank. He crossed his arms, leaned against the wall and rested his head.

"Did you hear me?" He scratched his chin and stared at the ceiling. I think he might have been rolling his eyes.

"I heard you. It's fine." I waited for him to elaborate, but he said nothing. He was cold. I thought about all that I'd shared with him yesterday. We were friendly at the park. He was sweet with Emily. Now he leaned against a wall, unmoved and blank. He didn't care.

Another thought occurred to me and a chill rolled down my back. Was he involved? I was so confused. I stepped back from him.

He leaned forward and furrowed his brow, "Where are you going?" I took another step back and turned.

"I need to get another resident for our next activity," I muttered. I stumbled as I moved down the hall.

CHAPTER 26

As Tai Chi ended, Alicia and I rearranged the room in silence. She hummed to herself and popped something in her mouth. I wanted to slap her snack from her hand. I finished my row and considered pressing Alicia for more information. She kept working on her row, continuing to hum.

"Something bothering you, Denise?" Alicia asked. If I hadn't seen the broach this morning, I might have received her question as an innocent inquiry. She reached out to touch my shoulder.

I gritted my teeth. "I think that I'm going to be sick." I didn't add, "if you touch me." She quickly retracted her hand. I fanned my face with my hand.

"You better sit down. I'll go get the residents." She retreated from me. I sunk into one of the chairs. For a little while I was alone, but the room began to fill again. I tried to remember what the next activity was until I saw him.

"Hello, Denise; you look well." Rev. Foucher looked down at me through his wire-rimmed glasses. Every hair in place, shirt and suit pressed to perfection. I looked down at myself. My ponytail had half fallen out and I tucked the hair behind my ear. I hadn't tucked in my black cotton shirt. It hung over a long floral skirt. This morning when I'd chosen the outfit I thought it felt comfortable and looked okay, but I noticed the hem was torn on one side. I'd definitely forgotten to put on lipstick as well. This day was going from lousy to hell-in-a-hand-basket. The man loomed over me.

I immediately stood up, knocking over my chair. I turned around to pick it up and pushed two other chairs out of place. I rearranged them and finally turned around and looked Rev. Foucher in the eye.

I hadn't seen the man for three months. I actually felt a little sick to my stomach. Anyone watching the scene would have thought that he projected the most fatherly care. He had perfected the look in a tweed coat and loafers. He turned his head slightly to the side, wrinkled his brow, and offered a slight smile through his grey beard. I recognized the look as his "pastoral care stare." He often looked at you that way when he was either about to fire you or ask you for something. Since he'd already fired me, I guess he must have wanted something.

"Rev. Foucher, how are you?" I asked. I squeezed my hands behind my back so I wouldn't shake. I still felt so angry and insecure about myself around him.

"I'm doing really well. St. Christopher's continues to flourish, praise God!" He smiled, revealing his pearly whites. I guess he got them bleached, again. The contrast of white against grey startled me and I giggled. I covered it with a cough, but he immediately stopped talking. Oh dear, I had committed the unpardonable sin of interrupting Rev. Foucher when he was showing off.

"Do you need anything for the service, Rev. Foucher?" I ignored his disappointed look. When I'd worked for him, no one was allowed to interrupt him, especially if he was bragging about something.

"No," he answered. I turned around and began to walk away.

"Wait!" he snapped. I turned back and looked at him. He took a breath and the "pastoral care stare" returned. "I called you this weekend, Denise, and you did not return my call." He spoke to me like a disappointed father. I thought for a moment how I would respond.

In the past, if I'd felt that someone was disappointed in me, I would crumble. Immediately, I would apologize, even if I felt I didn't do anything wrong. In the past, I thought apologizing would repair the relationship. I recognized that he wanted me to apologize, but in that moment, I realized that I hadn't done anything wrong. I didn't want this relationship.

"You said in your message, I should call back when I was available. I'm not available," I answered. The room behind us was filling up. Rev. Foucher flared his nostrils.

"If you're available right now, I'd like to speak to you about something important." I could tell that the words pained him. Was he going to apologize to me? Now I was curious.

I tightened the grip on my fingers behind my back. I straightened my spine and directed my attention to him. I waited, looking him in the eye.

"Denise, I know how foolish you feel about quitting at St. Christopher's. We certainly miss your youth and exuberance. I can see that you're just floundering, which is terrible for someone as talented as you. I want you to know that I forgive you." He reached one palm towards me, and it took everything within me to resist slapping his hand. I think he must have sensed that I might hit him so he quickly withdrew his hand and dropped it by his side.

I was flabbergasted! I wasn't sure how to respond to him. Indeed, I felt foolish about my final encounter with Rev. Foucher at St. Christopher's. For the last three months I had replayed the conversation with him over in my mind. I'd questioned my judgment. Why had I told him I was interested in doing something else? My sister reminded me that technically he could construe what I'd said as a clear resignation, but how come it wasn't clear to me? I remained quiet.

"You might not realize this, but St. Christopher's is entering into an exciting time in its ministry..." Wait, was he about to give me a sales pitch? "We're starting work on our bi-centennial campaign..." He was ready to make his pitch.

I raised my hand. "Wait, why are you telling me this, Ronald?" I used his first name because I knew how much he hated to be called by his first name by someone he considered "younger" or lesser than him. He wanted to be called either "Reverend" or "Father."

He cleared his throat. "I'm telling you this because I know that you care about St. Christopher's. I also know that you and your family have deep roots in the New Orleans' community, especially your mother Margaret." He stood very still for a moment.

"But why are you telling me?" My patience was growing thin and it was becoming difficult to keep the anger from my voice. The room was filling up. The Tuesday congregation were either listening to our exchange or they were asleep. Either way, the room was silent. I waited for his reply.

"He's saying it because he wants you to use your connections and your resources to help him ask for money from your mother's friends." The familiar voice behind me answered my question. I swung around and looked down at Louise through her coke bottle lenses. I could have burst into tears I was so happy to see her.

"It isn't like that, exactly," he answered Louise with exasperation. "This could be an opportunity for her to help St. Christopher's."

"Oh, so you'll pay her to spy and feed you information?" Louise moved around me and stood on my right. She stepped a little in front of me, as if she was preparing to strike him.

"Don't be so dramatic," he growled, and regained his composure "Besides, I'm sure Denise wouldn't mind. She has nothing else to do. This gives her a chance to finally make a difference and feel better about her foolish mistake." His words felt like a slap in the face. My cheeks felt hot and I could tell that red was creeping up my neck. I could feel the tears. I released a ragged sigh.

"She does make a difference," I heard another familiar voice. Rev. Foucher turned towards the door behind him. My mother leaned on the frame, her arms crossed, and her face was filled with disgust.

Rev. Foucher's shoulders slumped. My mother walked into the room and sat at a chair in the front row, placing her purse next to her chair. "Shouldn't we be getting started with church?" she asked to no one in particular.

Louise pulled on my arm, "Denise, help me find my sweater." With that, she led me from the room before I burst into tears. In the hallway, Louise dug in her purse and handed me a tissue package.

"We need to talk," she said, as she led me to her suite. She took her keys from her pocket and opened the door. "Take a seat, honey." I found my usual perch on the couch and as usual, she pulled out the sherry. This time, my glass was a champagne flute.

"Isn't that a little much, Louise?" I asked as I took the glass from her hand. My hands were still shaking from earlier.

"Isn't that pompous ass a little much, Denise?" she deadpanned. We both laughed. I laughed so hard that I almost spilled the sherry, but I was able to take a sip.

When she settled into her chair, holding her glass between her two hands, I finally spoke, "I thought that something had happened to you this morning. I couldn't find you anywhere. I was really worried." With that, I felt the tears come again.

She sweetly smiled. "Denise, you really are so sweet. I should have told you last night that I had a doctor's appointment this morning. The van took me at about 7 to Touro, but my appointment was not until 9." I slumped into her couch. I felt relief. I thought back to my earlier suspicions about Jason. I must have sounded ridiculous.

"I found out something, Denise."

I leaned forward to listen. I put down my champagne flute. Her tone was sorrowful. I wondered if she'd gotten bad news at her doctor's appointment. For that matter, I didn't even know that much about her health in general.

"Are you okay, Louise?" I wasn't sure I could take any additional emotional upheaval this day.

Louise shook her head, "No, I'm fine. The police discovered who hit Tina Moore and drove away."

I was shocked. This was also troubling news.

"How did you find out? Who was it?" I asked. I realized that I hadn't watched the news last night or this morning.

Louise sipped her sherry and let the questions linger. "He was just a young man driving too fast on Broadway with too much alcohol in his system. It was an accident. She fell into the street in front of him and he didn't stop in time. He panicked. I guess he could no longer live with the guilt of hitting and killing someone. He wrote a note and then..." She just stopped talking. I took a gulp of my sherry and gagged slightly.

"Oh, that's tragic." I sunk back into the couch. I picked up my sherry and sipped again. The stuff tasted terrible, but I could use a drink. "So, now what?"

"That's it, Denise," she answered. She sounded defeated.

"What do you mean?" I readjusted in my seat so I could see Louise's expression.

"I guess that we're finished with our investigation. I was wrong. No one here killed Tina. It's finished." She swallowed her whole glass and then got up, went to the kitchen, and returned with another full glass.

"But what about the thefts? I think that I might have proof. It may not be related to Tina's death, but still..." I was shocked. Louise was defeated. She just shrugged her shoulders. Just then, I knew why my mother hated when people shrugged.

"Louise," I pleaded. She took another swig of her sherry and coughed a little. She wiped her lips with the back of her hand. She put down her glass and straightened in her chair.

"Okay, Denise, what did you find out?" Her tone was flat. I stared at my friend. She shook her head. "I'm sorry. I dragged you into this and now I'm abandoning you before we see this investigation through. Please tell me what you found."

I put down my drink and stood. "First, tell me where you pearl broach is," I said with an air of confidence I hadn't felt for months. She scrunched her face while thinking. Rising from her chair, she entered her bedroom while I waited smugly.

"Hey!" she shouted from her bedroom and ran out. "Where's my pearl broach?"

"I saw Alicia wearing it today. And so did Ms. Cramer." I was triumphant for a moment. I then realized that while I knew where Louise's broach was, I wasn't sure just how we'd get it back.

"Well, I can't believe it. Alicia seems so nice," Louise spoke as if in a daze. She sat on the edge of her chair and took another swig of sherry. This time she coughed so hard that she spat it out. "Oh, excuse me, I guess I can't handle my sherry like I used to." She went to the kitchen for a dish rag and wiped up her mess. "We better go see Ms. Cramer."

"Yes, but I don't think that Alicia is doing this alone. Yesterday Alicia's boyfriend and another aide threatened me after I went to security about Lydia's watch. Or at least I think they were threatening me." Louise considered my words. "We still don't know everyone who's involved."

"True, but we have to start somewhere. Let's go talk to Ms. Cramer." Louise picked up her purse and we headed to Ms. Cramer's office.

CHAPTER 27

"Are you sure that was Ms. Butler's broach?" Ms. Cramer asked from behind her desk. Louise and I sat in the folding chairs across from her in her tiny office.

"Ms. Cramer, you saw the broach this morning too. I'm sure that you recognize it because Louise, I mean, Ms. Butler wore it to my party a few weeks ago and you commented on it," I answered. Ms. Cramer leaned back in her chair and crossed her arms over her chest. A flicker of recognition moved across her face like she was remembering something.

"I thought I recognized it," she muttered, turning her chair from us so that she now faced a wall of filing cabinets. She chewed her thumb nail and then looked at it and grimaced. She turned back to us. "Are you sure that it's the same? A lot of jewelry looks the same. Have you looked really carefully for your broach, Ms. Butler?"

"Yes, I've looked, Ms. Cramer, and my broach is missing from my jewelry box." Louise pronounced each word slowly and carefully as if she was giving directions to a tourist. The two women glared at each other.

"Could you have misplaced the item, Ms. Butler? Often times older people misplace items." Ms. Cramer asked her automatic response, then she looked down at her desk and rearranged her papers. Louise must have won this round of the staring contest.

"Ms. Cramer, it *was* Louise's broach. You saw it. I saw it," I interjected. Ms. Cramer rolled her eyes and nodded her head.

"Did you give her the broach, Ms. Butler? Perhaps you've forgotten about giving her the broach." I thought that Louise might reach across the desk and slap Ms. Cramer at that point, but she restrained herself and merely shook her head.

"Fine. I'll take care of this." She lifted the receiver on the phone and spoke with someone. She hung up the phone. "I'll be right back. Stay here." With that, she left the office.

Louise and I sat for about ten minutes and were about to leave when Ms. Cramer returned. She had one of the guards. She directed him to stand next to her desk. A few minutes later, Alicia entered Ms. Cramer's office. She looked like a deer in headlights.

"Alicia, would you please show us the broach you were wearing this morning before Tai Chi?" Ms. Cramer asked quietly. She stood behind her desk while Alicia stood behind Louise and me. Both Louise and I craned our necks to see Alicia.

The office felt hot and airless while we waited for Alicia to reveal the broach. She delicately unclipped it from her blouse and placed it on Ms. Cramer's desk. Ms. Cramer looked pointedly at Louise and then the object. Louise reached forward and picked up her broach. Without a word, everyone in the office knew to whom the broach belonged.

"Ms. Butler and Ms. Reed, would you please excuse us?" Ms. Cramer dismissed us. Louise clutched her broach and held it to her chest. She looked down at her broach and up at Alicia as we walked out the door.

CHAPTER 28

As Louise and I left Ms. Cramer's office, there was a group of staff members milling around the lobby. Melinda, one of the housekeepers, was speaking with pimple face. The two glared at me. I quickly moved to the elevators.

I only had an hour left on my shift. I kept busy, avoiding eye contact with any of the staff. I noticed that some of the housekeeping staff would whisper and look at me. When I walked past them, they would stop talking. The word got around quickly about Alicia. I wasn't sure what had happened to her, but I had a good idea. When the clock struck one, I raced to the sign-out sheet at the reception desk and ran to my car.

While I started my car, I heard a knock on my window. I jumped and saw Jason. I rolled the window down. "You scared me!"

He leaned into the car and put both hands on my door. "I didn't mean to scare you. I see that you found Louise. Is everything okay?"

"Yes, I found her. I guess she found me, actually." I smiled when I thought of her rescuing me earlier that day. He looked back at the building and then looked at me.

"I heard Alicia got fired. Tell me what happened." He leaned closer into the window. I could smell that wonderful mint and leather. How could he still smell that good after half a day?

"Alicia stole Louise's broach. I recognized it when I saw Alicia wearing it today. Louise identified it as hers." I stated the facts. Jason looked back at the building.

"Okay, you better get going. Thanks." With that, he abruptly walked away. I watched him through my windshield. He jogged to the entrance of the building and pulled out his cellphone. I pulled out of the parking lot.

I got home quickly and kicked off my shoes. I had a few hours to kill before picking up Emily. I thought that now would be a good time to read Carrie's screenplay. I settled at the kitchen table and flipped open my laptop. I opened the file and began to read.

Her writing was fabulous. The story was a mystery with a heaping side of romance. I loved it! I was almost to the end. The villain was about to strike.

"Hello!" my mother bellowed from the doorway behind me. I jumped in my seat and yelped. She sat down in the kitchen chair next to me.

"I'm sorry I startled you. Were you reading something scary?" She leaned around to see my screen. I turned the computer so she could look. She read for a little while and then looked at me.

"What is that?" She was fascinated. She reached over and scrolled down the page, reading more.

"It's Carrie's screenplay. I'm almost finished reading it. I'm going to help her with some editing," I answered and turned the screen back towards me. My mother turned the screen back towards her. She took her glasses from her pocket and put them on, continuing to read. I cleared my throat.

She smiled sheepishly. "Sorry. It looks really interesting. May I look at it, when you're finished?"

"Sure, if you want to." She smiled tenderly at me. I was surprised that a murder mystery could cause this reaction in my mother.

"Uh, I wanted to talk to you about today." She took off her glasses and put them away. My mother was usually so sure, but at this moment she was nervous.

"Okay, Mom, what is it?" I closed the cover of the laptop and faced her. She reached over and took my hand.

"I saw what happened today with Rev. Foucher," She began. She chose her words carefully. Whatever she had to say demanded delicacy, and I wasn't sure if I wanted to hear them.

"I know, Mom, what you said was great." I tried to continue speaking, brush aside what had happened earlier. I was touched that she'd defended me, but I also felt a little embarrassed about the whole scene. She raised her hand to silence me. Pain swept across her face.

"Yes and what I said was true. You do make a difference. You have made a difference your whole life. I also know that you will always make a difference, in anything you do. When I heard that man degrade you and minimize what you've done and who you are, I felt so angry," she squeezed my hand a little too tightly and then let go.

"I felt angry too, Mom." Again she shushed me. She focused her gaze on me. The corners of her eyes were moist.

"Let me finish! I was angry at that man, but I was sad. I was sad because I wondered if you believed him. I was disappointed when you quit St. Christopher's. I worried that you wouldn't find anything else as good. Now I realize how wrong I was. You don't have to find anything 'as good' because you already have it. *You* are what is good." She patted my hand. I felt the tears building in my eyes.

She hopped up and walked to the sink. She wetted a paper towel and handed it to me. Again she took my hand and we sat quietly.

"Thanks, Mom." We both smiled at each other. She nodded her head.

"Hey, why don't we go to Slice tonight? I think we could use a good anchovy pizza." She stood up and headed for her room. She stopped at the doorway and turned to look at me. Again she smiled.

CHAPTER 29

That evening, the three of us wandered down the street to Slice on Magazine. My sister, brother-in-law and their four children joined us for dinner. We gorged ourselves on caprese salad and anchovy pizza. Emily tried a bite and opted to stick with her slice of pepperoni.

Our table was boisterous and loud and fun. When we finished, I pried Emily from her favorite cousin, James, and the three of us returned home. At the house, I finally looked at my phone. There were two messages from Louise.

I stepped into the bedroom and called her back. On the last ring, Louise answered with another sing-songy, "Hello!"

"Hello, Louise; it's Denise. I was calling you back," I replied. I wondered why I even bothered telling her my name when I knew full and well that she had caller id on her cellphone like everyone else in the Western Hemisphere.

"Denise, I'm so glad you called. I wanted to update you on what happened this afternoon." She waited a beat and started talking, "Ms. Cramer fired Alicia." I nodded my head.

"I kind of figured that out, Louise." I tried to reel in my sarcastic tone. I waved my hand next to the phone, aware that she could not see me make the motion.

Louise went on, ignoring my tone, "They escorted her out the back door. She just stood there with a cardboard box in her hands. Mabel Watkins watched from her balcony. Apparently, she was just bawling and bawling, saying 'it was a present' over and over again." I could hear the satisfaction in her voice. "But," and here her tone changed. I could hear worry creep in. "Nobody called the police."

"That can't be right, Louise. Surely Ms. Cramer called them. I'm sure there needs to be some sort of follow-up." I thought about what I'd said.

"Maybe, but Ms. Cramer didn't mention it when she spoke to me this afternoon. She told me that Alicia insisted that the broach was a gift from someone, but she would not say who. She thanked me for bringing the 'misappropriation' to her attention and that she was taking care of it."

"Well, if she said she was taking care of it, I'm sure that means that she alerted the authorities about this." Something nagged at me. Certainly Alicia was wearing Louise's broach, but that didn't sound like the actions of someone trying to conceal a theft. She seemed proud of the pin and thought it was hers. On the other hand, she might have thought no one would have realized the theft. She could have kept it under her smock without notice or thought that maybe no one would recognize the broach except for Louise.

Surely if she was a thief, she wasn't working alone. What about pimple face and the brick wall? They were definitely up to something shady. Were they all working together? What would happen with them? "Did she say anything about anyone else getting fired or leaving? Those two jerks who threatened me?"

"I didn't ask. I should have, though." I heard the doubt in Louise's voice. Now I was really uneasy. Louise could be targeted by them, if they were still there.

"Louise, why don't you call the police? You can tell them what's going on. I went by this morning and they can follow up." I hoped she heard the urgency in my voice.

"I don't know, Denise. Will they even listen to me?" I thought for a moment and retrieved my purse. I dug through until I found the card that Officer Perez had handed me.

"I think I know someone who will talk to you. I spoke with her. Her name is Officer Perez, and I have her cell." I waited for Louise's reply. I could hear her moving around her suite.

"Well, give me the number and I'll call her right now." Relief flooded me. I knew that Officer Perez could help, even if only to add to my original report. I heard Louise rummage around for a pen. "Okay, I'm ready."

I rattled off the seven digits. She repeated the numbers twice. I made her promise to call me after she spoke with Officer Perez and then I hung up.

I waited for thirty minutes. I probably reread the same chapter in my book four times. I slipped into the kitchen for a snack and settled on one more slice of anchovy pizza. I would probably regret it at 2 a.m., but I was willing to take the risk.

At 10, I decided to call it a night when my cellphone rang. I didn't recognize the number but I picked up anyway. The line cracked a little and then I heard the phone fall. Someone fumbled with the phone and then spoke, "I hope nothing happens to your friend."

I didn't quite comprehend what the person was saying, so I said, "Hello?"

"I said I hope nothing happens to your friend." I understood the caller, but somehow I thought it might be better to pretend not to. You never know when someone has a wrong number, besides if you're going to harass me over the phone, I get to pretend I cannot understand you. My other super power is annoyance.

"Hello," I smirked, as I heard the caller swear.

"She can't hear me. Man, this stupid lady has a cheap phone." He spoke to someone else in the room. The caller hung up. I finally recognized pimple face's voice. I looked at my cellphone like I was holding a snake.

I dropped it on the couch and was just about to go climb under my bed when I was struck. Was he talking about Louise? Was Louise in danger?

I grabbed my phone and immediately dialed Louise's number. The phone rang and then went to voicemail. I called Riverview. After what felt like an eternity of rings, the operator picked up the phone.

I explained that I needed to speak with Ms. Butler. It was an emergency. The operator put me on hold. The lined beeped and I heard a very tired, very loud Louise on the other end.

"Who is this? Do you have any idea what time it is?" Louise was cross. Super cross, but she sounded unharmed, for now.

"Louise, it's Denise. Are you okay? Are you safe?" I shouted into the phone.

"I'm fine, Denise! Stop shouting at me! I called Officer Perez, but I got her voicemail. After that, I went to bed." Louise was exasperated.

"You said you'd call me after you called Officer Perez," I replied angrily and plopped down on the edge of my bed. I felt exhausted.

"I promised to call after I 'spoke' to Officer Perez. I only got her voicemail, Denise," Louise explained barely maintaining a civil tone. "You didn't need to have Lawrence and Claude come pound on my door and hand me their phone."

Who are Lawrence and Claude? I wondered. I never noticed any men working at the reception desk.

"Lawrence Nelson and Claude Peterson, they're the security at Riverview."

So Mr. Itchy Crotch and Cat Video Guy had names? Of course, that made sense.

"Denise, I'm going to bed. I will call Officer Perez again in the morning. I will see you tomorrow. Good night." Before I could say anymore, she hung up.

I stared at the phone in my hand. I gritted my teeth. I could not believe that she blew me off when her safety might be on the line. I wanted to tell her about the call I'd received, but she wouldn't let me get a word in edgewise.

On the other hand, she had the two security guards, however inept, with her at this moment. Surely, she'd be safe this evening, and tomorrow morning she'd call Officer Perez and make her report. She was safe in her suite.

I stood up and stretched. I paced the room while I contemplated whether or not I should call the police about the call. How would I explain this threat? Would they be able to do anything?

I picked up Officer Perez's number from my bed side table. I would call her. I looked at the time. It was 10:45. I might be able to catch her before she fell asleep.

I dialed the number and waited while the phone rang. I expected to get her voicemail, but she picked up and coughed, "Perez here."

"Hi, Officer Perez, this is Denise Reed. I spoke to you early this morning?" I thought she would remember me. I could hear her yawn. I had awakened her.

"Yes, Ms. Reed, how can I help you?" She sounded more alert now. I perched on the edge of my bed.

"I think that someone threatened my friend this evening. They called and said that: they hoped nothing happened to my friend." I could hear Officer Perez sigh. Somehow I could tell she was shaking her head.

"Ms. Reed, have you called 911 about this?" She asked matter of fact.

"No, I wasn't sure if I should." Again, I could tell she was shaking her head. She was getting frustrated with me.

"Ms. Reed, there's nothing that I can do about this. You should probably call 911, but I'm not sure what they can do about it either, really," she answered honestly.

"But what about my friend?" I asked.

"Have you contacted her?" she asked.

"Yes, I called Louise about ten minutes ago. She seems okay. The security guards at Riverview are with her." As I said the words out loud, I realized how ridiculous this all sounded. Louise was fine.

"If she has security with her, I'm sure that she's fine." I heard Officer Perez shift around. I realized that she must be in bed. "Are you talking about Louise Butler?"

"Yes."

"Yeah, she left me a message tonight. I just tried to call her a little while ago, but her phone must be turned off." I nodded my head in agreement. She yawned loudly, "Excuse me."

I heard in the background a man's voice: "Who you talking to, babe?" She shushed him, "It's a case, sweetie, go back to sleep." I heard a little giggle and a kiss.

"I'm sorry I woke you, Officer Perez." I felt foolish bothering her in bed with her husband.

"It's okay, Ms. Reed. You have a good night." I heard her yawn again.

"You too. Good night." I hung up and turned off my phone. I arranged myself in my bed, turned out my bedside lamp, and fell asleep.

CHAPTER 30

The next morning, I felt slow and groggy, as I padded into the kitchen to pour myself some coffee. The newspaper lay folded at the table. I knew that my mother had already read it, like she did every morning after her walk and with her coffee.

"Are you finished with the paper?" I shouted. I knew that she was finished with it, but I still felt I should ask. My mother shouted her reply from the shower.

I opened the paper to the metro section. I scanned the articles looking for anything about Tina Moore's accident. I found the story on the last page, near the bottom and only five lines.

The story gave a quick explanation: "The New Orleans Police Department announces they have completed their investigation into the death of Tina Moore, 24. Theo Elliot, age 20, struck and killed Moore on the evening of September 21st around 6:30 p.m. Elliot admitted in a letter to being intoxicated and unable to stop, striking Moore who had fallen into Broadway Avenue. He then fled the scene. The discovery about Moore's death occurred when officers responded to a disturbance at Elliot's apartment." That was it.

I closed the paper. Emily ran into the kitchen and pulled on my arm. I needed to get her ready and fed for pre-school. I wondered who was getting Brandon and Bryce ready this morning, probably their grandmother.

"What are you thinking about, Denise?" My mom entered the room and immediately opened the refrigerator. She pulled out some eggs and a few other items, preparing her breakfast.

"Something I read in the paper." She wrinkled her forehead at me and returned to her preparation. She quickly whipped together an omelet faster than I could get a cereal box from the cabinet for Emily.

"Must have been something troubling; you're frowning." My mother pointed out from the stove. She flipped her omelet onto a plate in one smooth motion. She settled in next to me.

"There was a story about Tina Moore," I said. Her expression was quizzical as she took her first bite.

"Oh, yes, the young woman from Riverview, poor thing fell into the street and was hit by a car?" She popped another bite in her mouth. I shook my head. I looked over at Emily while she swirled the Cheerios in her milk.

"Emily, you need to hurry up and eat," I reminded her. "What can I say, the story is terrible and I'm not sure its conclusion is all that comforting." My mother nodded in agreement. I took a bite of my cereal.

"Sad all around. The young man was too drunk to stop when he saw her fall in the street." She tsked and took another bite. I bit into my Cheerios.

"Wait, what did you just say?" I put down my spoon and tried to replay her words.

"I said that it was sad also because the young man was unable to stop when Tina fell." At that, Emily stood up at her seat and dramatically fell to the floor.

"Like that, Mommy?" Emily beamed at me. I pointed to her seat and she climbed into her chair, resuming the Cheerios' race around her bowl.

"Yes," I said absently. I picked up the newspaper and turned to the story. I reread the story three times. Something nagged at me about the whole story. I thought about Tina in her casket and her bruised face.

"How did she fall?" I stood up, spilling cereal all over my lap. I grabbed a dish towel and started to wipe the front of my pajama bottoms.

"Denise? What are you talking about?" She hopped up from her seat, taking my bowl and her plate to the sink. She reached under the sink for some spray and paper towels.

I looked down at the mess I'd made. "Emily, you need to hurry up. Mommy has to get to work!" Emily looked up and slowly took a bite. She immediately began shoveling the cereal in when she saw my expression.

My mother stopped her cleaning and examined me. "What is it, Denise?" I helped her pick up the stray Cheerios and began tossing them into the garbage can.

"Just wondering, that's all." I smiled at my mother. I needed to hurry because I had some questions.

CHAPTER 31

I arrived at Riverview with 15 minutes to spare. I hoped that would give me enough time. I signed in at the reception desk. I smiled at the receptionist.

"Is Ms. Cramer in?" The young woman picked up her phone and spoke briefly. She waved me behind the desk. I tapped on Ms. Cramer's door.

"Come in!" she chirped. I opened the door and discovered Ms. Cramer standing at a file cabinet. She pushed the drawer closed. "Please, have a seat, Denise. What can I do for you today?"

She moved to her position behind the desk. She folded her hands on top of her desk. I examined the woman. This morning she wore a lavender suit with a patterned blouse. I saw my opening.

"What a great color, Ms. Cramer. Lavender is so lovely, don't you think? Or is it purple?" I asked innocently. Immediately, Ms. Cramer smiled. She leaned back in her chair.

"Thank you, Denise. I would call this lavender. I love this suit. I always get compliments on it," she answered proudly. I nodded approvingly. "So, why are you here?"

"I'm sorry. I'm so distracted this morning. That beautiful color reminds me of orchids. I just have to say it." I beamed at Ms. Cramer. She sighed. I could tell she was growing impatient.

"I saw the same color orchids at Tina Moore's visitation. Did you send those flowers, Ms. Cramer?" I asked innocently. She blanched, but recovered quickly.

"Yes, I remember ordering some flowers for the service. It was on behalf of Riverview." She rearranged some files on her desk. She began tapping a pen.

"That was the largest spray at the visitation. You should have seen it. Purple orchids and white roses, the fragrance filled that whole room. What a grand gesture. Did you know that purple was Tina Moore's favorite color?" I asked.

Ms. Cramer shifted in her chair, pulling at the bottom of her jacket. "I guess I had even more in common with Tina than I thought. Denise, is there a point to this? I'm really busy and you should be starting your shift."

"Did you know that lavender or purple is used during Lent and other penitential times during the church year?" Ms. Cramer straightened in her chair and scooted forward. I could see her jaw tighten and relax. I continued: "I want to talk about the day you spoke with me about helping Ms. Butler deal with Tina Moore's death."

"What about it?" she asked through a clenched jaw. She moved her hands to her lap. I leaned forward in my folding chair.

"When you and I spoke, you told me about Tina's accident. I'd like you to tell me about that day again." I examined her as she gazed around the room, avoiding eye contact.

"Why would I do that? I have a lot of work to do, Denise." Ms. Cramer stood up and motioned to the door.

"Because the police found the person who hit Tina Moore," I answered. Ms. Cramer shrugged her shoulders. I continued: "But there are still questions." Ms. Cramer dropped her arm to her side.

"What questions? I saw the article too. That young man hit her and drove off." Ms. Cramer remained standing.

"When you and I spoke, you told me that you fired Tina Moore that day, is that correct?" Ms. Cramer sank into her seat. She looked down at her lap.

"Yes, I fired her that day." She examined her nails, picking at her index finger.

I shifted my weight and focused on her, "What did she do after you dismissed her, Ms. Cramer?"

"At the end of her shift, she gathered her belongings, and Lawrence escorted her from the building, through the back entrance." Ms. Cramer returned my stare. A wall went up behind her eyes.

"Why did you dismiss her, Ms. Cramer?" I pressed.

"I cannot discuss that. It's confidential." I shook my head. "Are we finished here?"

"Not quite. What happened to her after she left the building, Ms. Cramer?" I asked.

"You know what happened. She was hit by a car," Ms. Cramer shot back.

"Yes, she was, but I wonder how that happened. How did she fall into the street again?" I waited for her reply.

Ms. Cramer let out a frustrated breath, "It's what I said before: she tripped on a root near the curb and fell into the street. Then he hit her." She almost slammed her fist on the desk.

"How did you know that she tripped on a root?" I dropped the mic. Ms. Cramer turned red. Her mouth dropped open and her hand covered her mouth. She sucked in breath.

She tried to cover her tracks. "I think the police said something like that. I believe I heard the police say that," she insisted, hopeful that I would believe her. I stretched back in my chair. I held her gaze.

"No, Ms. Cramer, they did not say anything about that. Frankly, they don't seem that concerned with that part. I wonder what caused her to trip. Why wasn't she paying attention to where she was walking?" I continued. She shook her head. Her eyes pleaded for me to stop.

"I didn't do anything," she said. She held her lips tightly together.

"I know you didn't hit her with your car, but how did you know how she tripped?" I reached a hand across the desk to her. She took my hand. I pleaded, "Please tell me what happened."

Her face took on the appearance of an upside down kidney bean and the tears started to roll. I let her cry. No other sound exited her body. She shook from her tears, but she was silent. Finally, she picked up a tissue from somewhere in her desk and blew her nose.

"I had fired Tina that day. I have to admit it. I didn't like her that much, but she was really good at her job. She was on time, professional and respectful. Everyone loved her. She came to me the morning after Mrs. Lees died. She reported that she suspected someone had stolen a necklace, some sort of Wedgewood pendant, from Mrs. Lees." Ms. Cramer rolled her eyes, "She was determined that we investigate. I tried to talk this through with her. There might have been other explanations."

"Like what?" I asked.

"Like? I don't know. Maybe Mrs. Lees' daughter took the necklace with her? Maybe she got rid of it a while back?" She gauged my expression, and sunk into her chair. "Look, someone might have taken the necklace, but we would never be able to prove who. For that matter, Riverview couldn't call the police in. It would ruin our reputation and we would still never find

Mrs. Lees' necklace. I told her that I would look into it."

"Which meant that you actually would not look into it," I stated. She shook her head and blew her nose again. "So, why did you fire her?"

"She said to me: 'That's not good enough' and marched out of my office, like she was a knight in shining armor. I wasn't sure what she meant, but I knew it was a threat. She was going to Dr. Martin. She went on her shift, so I went to the security department." She laughed. "Of course, those two dolts had nothing on camera because once again they hadn't turned them on. This worked to my advantage. I found her going into his office. She told him what she told me, but there was nothing to substantiate what she'd said. So, in the meeting, I insinuated that maybe she was stealing."

I felt a little sick to my stomach. Ms. Cramer became very still and very quiet. "Please go on," I encouraged her. I sat at the edge of my chair.

"So, I fired her. I had Lawrence collect her belongings and leave the building. It wasn't quite the end of her shift, so she was just sitting outside the gate, with her box, crying. When I finished work, I went outside. She was still there, still crying, but she was talking on her phone. I felt really bad about how it went down. I thought that I was going to get fired because of the security department, but their stupid mistake actually saved my butt." The phone buzzed, but she pressed a button to silence it.

"So, I went to speak with her. She looked at me like I was an alligator. She got up, took her stuff and started walking away. I called out to her, and she shouted back: 'Leave me alone!' I could hear her crying and she started running from me, so I chased her down the block. I caught up with her near the bus stop. I grabbed her arm. I turned her around. I just wanted to talk to her. She yanked her arm away, turned around and tripped over the root and fell into the street. I tried to help her up when he hit her. It happened so fast." She was almost whispering, "He didn't stop. I was just frozen there. Then I just ran away. I left her. Nobody saw me."

"Could she have still been alive when you left?" I asked. I wasn't sure if I wanted to know the answer.

"Yes. She was alive." She relived the moment. She shut her eyes to drive it away. "How did you know, Denise?"

"You told me about the roots." I thought this was pretty obvious. She nodded.

"No, how did you know?" I understood the question now.

"You told me. You felt guilty when we spoke before, that was clear. The huge funeral spray shouted: 'I'm making up for something.' I thought it was about the firing at first, but there was something very personal about the gesture, all that lavender." She looked down at her suit and shrugged.

"It *is* my favorite color," she bit her lip as she spoke.

"It was Tina Moore's favorite color too." She shook her head. "It's also a penitential color, like I said before. We repent in Lent, and we ask for forgiveness. All that purple is a reminder." Ms. Cramer started straightening her desk and cleared her throat.

"So, what do I do now?" She didn't look at me as she was asking. She moved a few things on her desk.

I considered her question. She might not have caused Tina Moore's death, but she participated in the circumstance that led to her death. She hadn't stopped to render aid and instead a young woman lay dying in the street, alone.

"I think that you need to tell the truth. Talk to the police, talk to a lawyer and tell the truth. Tina Moore deserves that and so do you." I stood up and stretched my arms at my side. I was not sure what to do with this story, but I did know it was not mine to tell.

As I was walking from the room, I heard her pick up the phone behind me. I turned back briefly and she waved. Something told me that this day was probably going to be her final day at Riverview.

CHAPTER 32

My shift was exhausting, especially without any
help. I set up chairs, escorted residents, filled out
paperwork and the time flew by. At one, I made my
way to the employee lunch room. Once again, I forgot
my lunch and loathed buying a $2 bag of off-brand
Doritos. I noticed that the other employees were
avoiding me and I really couldn't blame them. I figured
that many had heard that I'd accompanied Louise to
report Alicia's theft.

Finally, someone had enough nerve to approach me,
Melinda from housekeeping. She marched over to my
table and stood across the table from me. She looked
down and then leaned forward on the table and tapped
her perfectly painted sparkly nails. She cleared her
throat.

"What do you think you're doing?" I bit one of my
chips. Nope, these definitely were not a Doritos knock
off. She looked pretty fierce. Her hair was in a tight
slick bun and even her small hoop earrings appeared to
shake. She pointed a finger right at my face.

"What do you mean?" I asked, abandoning my
chips. They really needed to invest in the snack
machines at Riverview. I returned her glare.

"You're getting people fired! Everyone knows you
got Alicia fired for no reason and now the police are
here for Cramer? What are you doing?" I didn't realize
that the police had come. I weighed what I'd tell this
woman. I didn't know her very well, but this was one of

those cases that saying "none of your business" might get me smacked across the face.

"I went with Ms. Butler to report a theft. Alicia was wearing Ms. Butler's broach," I spoke quietly and directly. Melinda stood straight up. I could see her clench and release her jaw.

"Mickey said you had it out for Alicia and wanted her job," she stated matter of factly. She folded her arms across her chest.

"No." I straightened in my chair and put both hands on the table. "Who's Mickey?" I asked. I wondered if after this encounter I would need to seek out this Mickey and ask why he was spreading rumors about me.

"Her boyfriend, duh." Melinda answered as if I was an imbecile. I tapped my hands on the table, waiting for what she wanted to say next. She shifted her weight from one leg to another and then she stopped and sucked in a breath. She glared down at me and then her eyes widened as if she'd just discovered something. "Oh," she thought about it and then asked, "Do you want her job?" Her demeanor shifted from hostile to curious.

"Melinda, I don't know and no one has offered it to me," I answered truthfully. I guess there was an opening and it was full-time. In all the excitement of the investigation, I really hadn't thought about what I was doing at Riverview as a true career option. "Are you thinking about pursuing the position?" I asked her. Her jaw dropped. She vigorously shook her head no.

She sat down across from me. She leaned a little closer. "Someone told me that Ms. Cramer told the police that she had something to do with Tina's death, is that true?" I held my confidence, but Melinda read my silence as confirmation. She wiped a tear from her eye. She whispered, "You figured that out, didn't you?"

I shrugged my shoulders and she finally smiled. Her face relaxed and she let out a little laugh and then just as suddenly she became suspicious: "Are you a cop or something?" I shook my head no, and she smiled again, "Good."

I had the distinct feeling that Melinda was not finished with her questions, but my shift had ended. I looked down at my watch. She sat for a moment and motioned for my chips. I handed her the bag. "I'm sorry that I came at you like that. I really liked Alicia. I didn't think she was fooling around with that stuff."

"What stuff?" I asked innocently. She held a chip and considered whether she would take a bite. She popped it into her mouth and grimaced.

"You know, the thefts?" she answered. Obviously not satisfied with her judgment on the first bite, she took another, "Man, those things are terrible." She put down the bag.

"What about the thefts?" I pushed. Melinda leaned back in her chair. She scanned the room and licked her lips.

She leaned in again and spoke so softly that I could barely hear her, "Look, we all know about it. Stuff comes up missing all the time and nobody sees anything. You get me?" She seemed nervous. I looked around the room. A secretary from the front office parked at the table across the room.

Honestly, she didn't tell me anything that I didn't know already. "Uh huh?" She shook her head in frustration and looked around again. She motioned for me to lean closer, so I did.

"I said: 'Nobody sees anything.' Do you understand?" Could she have stated the obvious again? Of course, no one saw anything, which was why I was investigating and looking for proof. I thought that her eyes might pop out of her head if she rolled them that far back.

"Don't you get it?" She cocked her head a little to the left. I followed her gaze with my eyes. Her gaze landed on the camera mounted in the corner ceiling of the room.

"The cameras?" I looked straight at the camera. I wondered if old Mr. Itchy Crotch and Cat Video Guy were watching. I chuckled to myself realizing that they were probably in there looking at something obscene and nobody was watching. Nobody sees anything.

I pushed my chair back and shot up. "You mean..." I was about to point to the camera when Melinda grabbed my hand, digging in with her sparkly nails. "Ow!"

"Sit down! Geez, for a detective, you're pretty slow." Melinda folded her arms again. I sank into my seat and I thought about what she was implying. I knew that more than one person was involved in the thefts. I knew of at least three I'd safely consider criminals, but I hadn't considered what she was suggesting.

My mind returned to the present to her comment, "I'm not a detective." She rolled her eyes and stood up from the table. She tucked in her chair. Once again, she reached for a chip and tried it. Her face wrinkled in disgust. She headed for the door.

"Why did you tell me that?" She didn't turn around, but just lifted two fingers in a peace sign.

CHAPTER 33

I raced to Louise's suite and tapped on her door. I was so excited to speak with her and tell her what I'd found out. I wanted to find out how her conversation with Officer Perez had gone. I shifted my weight back and forth from foot to foot. I also really needed to pee.

I tapped again and listened. I touched the doorknob and considered whether or not I should twist it. I twisted the knob and the door opened. Louise tended to lock her suite, even when she was in it. This was unusual.

I pushed the door open wide and announced myself: "Louise, are you here? You left your door open." I stepped across the threshold and held my breath. I was struck with the odor.

Her apartment always smelled fresh, like bleach mixed with rosemary. Now it stunk of old liquor. I stepped a little farther into the apartment and I saw red on the white carpet. I almost shrieked in terror when I noticed her crystal decanter turned on its side next to the spill.

The sherry had splattered on the bottom of the couch and all over the carpet. I found the tray she used to carry the decanter and crystal glasses on the couch. One of Louise's slippers was also on the floor. Something had happened here. At the same time, I'd practically flipped out last night about Louise's safety and she had been snug in her bed.

I went into her bedroom. The bed clothes were tossed to one side, as if someone had been awakened only a moment before and had gone to the bathroom. I went to the bathroom. Nothing was amiss in there. This wasn't like Louise. Her place was always immaculate. She wouldn't have left a spill untended, and I suspected she was one of those folks who always made her bed.

I needed help and I needed it right now! I reached into the pocket of my brown cardigan for my phone. I remembered that I'd left it in my purse, in the car, locked in the trunk. I groaned when I realized it. I looked around the room for Louise's phone but it was nowhere to be found.

I ran from the apartment and looked down the hall for anyone. I decided to head for my car. I went to the elevator, but then I saw the Brick Wall. He stood right in front of the elevator. He sneered at me and began to walk in my direction. That's when I decided to run in the opposite direction.

"Come here!" he shouted behind me, but I didn't turn to respond. I've never been so grateful that this morning I'd put on my tennis shoes. I barreled down the hallway and I could hear his steps pounding behind me. I knew that a turn was coming and at the end of that hall were the back stairs.

He was right behind me. I could hear him puffing, but it might have been me. I felt one massive hand wrap around my shoulder and yank me backwards. At that moment, I realized one of the greatest benefits of my recent weight gain. I have substance—and significant substance falling backwards tends to knock over things around it.

I fell backwards and threw back my head. I heard a crack and a swear word as my head connected with his nose. My head throbbed. He was knocked off balance as well and I landed on top of him. For that brief moment, his vice grip released my shoulder and I sprung off him like an Olympic diver off a springboard.

I looked down at him on the floor just briefly. Blood spurted from his nose.

I continued running down the hallway and turned the corner. My head hurt but I kept moving as fast as I could. I turned the corner and could see the sign for the stairway. I almost reached my goal when I saw Jason. He'd just exited the apartment of one of the residents.

Before I could slow myself, I slammed into him. He let out a grunt, but he didn't topple over. Instead, he steadied me on my feet. "Denise, why are you running?"

I sucked in oxygen and huffed and puffed. I looked over my shoulder and the Brick Wall was nowhere to be seen. I touched my head and felt something wet. I looked down at my fingers. There was blood.

"You're hurt? Hang on, Denise!" Jason led me over to the wall and lowered me to the floor. He knelt next to me and examined my head. His fingers delicately felt my scalp. I winced as he pressed lightly on the spot. I would have huge goose egg. "What happened?"

His forehead wrinkled with concern. He held my cheeks in his hands and gently turned my head from side to side. He felt my shoulders and arms, carefully stretching each out to look for more injuries.

"I went to Louise's apartment and she wasn't there. Her place was a mess. I thought that something must have happened to her, so I was going to my car for my phone, but he was blocking the elevators and then he chased me." My teeth chattered from my nerves. I scanned the hallway, but my pursuer had still not turned the corner.

"Who was chasing you?" Jason asked. He locked his stare on me.

"The Brick Wall, that guy from the locker room! I tell you that he was waiting for me at that elevator. I didn't know what he was going to do," I squeaked out. I tried to slow down my breathing. My heart was still racing, but it was slowing down. My legs ached and my shoulder throbbed as well where the thug had grabbed me. I began to stand, but I felt wobbly.

"Wait a second!" Jason effortlessly stood and helped me from my seated position to stand up. I leaned against the wall. I needed to steady myself. I shook off his grip. "Wait, you need to slow down, you're hurt!" Jason protested. He actually looked angry. I felt weak and that I might vomit, but I needed to get away. I looked down the hallway. Rounding the corner was my attacker.

"I need to find help, Jason. I need to call the police or something." I started moving towards the stairwell, but Jason grabbed my hand. I pulled at my hand, but he held on. I would drag him down those steps, if I got there. Jason saw the fear in my eyes; he released my hand and turned around.

The Brick Wall clocked Jason square in the jaw. I watched Jason hit the floor and I shoved open the stairwell door, setting off an alarm in the building. I ran down the steps. It was only two floors. I heard the door above me open and slam shut.

I was finally to the first floor. I pushed the bar to open the door, but the door wouldn't move. The mechanism would unlock, but something was blocking the door from the outside. I pressed my non-throbbing shoulder into the door and it moved about an inch. I heard his feet pounding down the steps. He was getting closer.

Again, I shoved my shoulder into the door. This time it moved a few more inches, but I couldn't squeeze through the space. Why, oh why did I have to love pizza so much? I pushed and the door opened a little more, but still not enough. I could see through the crack that a hospital bed was blocking the door. I inwardly cursed the lazy fool who'd used that space for storage, ignoring the fire code. If I lived, I would report this to Dr. Martin. I let out a cry of frustration and again I felt a massive hand crush my hurt shoulder.

He swung me around. His other hand held a bloody piece of cloth to his nose. I could see the beginnings of bruises under his eyes. He looked like he was ready to pummel me, if only he could.

"You broke my nose!" he growled at me and began to pull me towards him. I winced from his grip. He was really digging his fingers into my shoulder. My impulse was to start apologizing profusely, but something overtook me.

Scientists talk about fight or flight. My usual unfortunate response to overwhelming terror—besides peeing on myself—is to freeze, but this time something marvelous and, not since I'd caught a stomach bug from Emily, happened. I projectile vomited all over him. It was the color of those terrible chips. It was glorious.

I think that I must have gotten some in his eyes and even his mouth. He let out a cry typical of a 12-year-old girl shrieking. He wiped at his eyes with the bloody rag. I immediately cackled like a witch. I was wracked with hysterical, Wicked Witch of the West laughter. He looked like he might burst into tears.

"I have plenty more where that came from," I announced and knocked his hand off my shoulder. He stepped back. I kicked him as hard as I could in his shin. He leaned over and grabbed his shin. I took my opportunity. I climbed the steps to the second floor. I was slower, but I had an unsteady stomach on my side. I never knew I would be so grateful for a weak gag reflex.

I shoved open the door. Another alarm rang. I ran down the hallway towards the elevators and hit the button. Again I pushed the button, waiting in agony. I watched down the hall, as he emerged from the stairwell. He limped towards me. He was heaving with fury.

The elevator opened and I ran in and hit the door *close* button just as he reached the doors. I heard him hit the closed doors. I pressed the first floor button and the elevator began its journey down. The door finally opened into the lobby. I sighed with relief when I saw who I thought was a police officer leaning against the reception desk.

"I need your help!" I ran right up to the man and grabbed a hold of his arm. I knew as soon as he turned from the desk that it was a mistake. He wasn't a police officer. He was Mr. Itchy Crotch, but today he wore a blue guard's uniform. I stepped unsteadily backwards. He gripped my upper arm.

"You don't look so good, Denise. I can help you. Let's go down to security." I tried to pull away. I could feel his fingers leaving bruises on my arm. I started to swing wildly and he caught my other hand. He calmly continued, "Louise is waiting for you." I sagged in his grip. I looked to the woman at reception, but she was turned away from me and on the telephone. "Let's go," he said under his breath.

We started walking down the hallway, towards the nursing unit. We were headed for security, and if I didn't think of something soon, I might be headed to my doom. I heard the elevator chime behind me and I looked back. A bloodied and vomit-encrusted thug exited. He walked with a slight limp towards us and stood on the other side of me. He refrained from touching me. For that, I smiled inwardly.

"Someone's going to see you. Let go of me," I growled, and pulled at my arm, hoping to break the grip.

"No one sees anything here," he answered without looking at me. He continued to drag me down the hallway.

I contemplated throwing myself on the floor. That usually worked for Emily, but what if they hurt Louise? We wandered quickly through the maze of hallways and we got to the security office. Mr. Itchy Crotch knocked on the door. The door opened an inch and then opened wider to let us in.

The guard shoved me into the room and we all crammed into the room together. Louise sat in a folding chair against one wall. Her small wrists were bound and she was still in her pink silk pajamas and robe. She sported a huge black eye. Cat Video Guy stood behind his desk again, a gun on the desk. The Brick Wall stood in front of the door while Mr. Itchy Crotch held my arm tightly. The three men looked at me.

"Where's the other one?" I asked. The three looked among each other. Mr. Itchy Crotch gave my arm a yank.

"He's still on shift," Cat Video Guy answered before Mr. Itchy Crotch shot him a glare.

"You don't ask the questions here. We do!" The other two nodded their heads. He shoved me into a chair next to Louise. I turned to her to check on her. Louise looked exhausted and probably drugged, but besides the black eye and tied wrists, she appeared mostly unharmed.

"What did you do to her?" I asked. I rubbed where he had squeezed my arm. My other shoulder throbbed.

"Gave her a tranquilizer; it can last all day." Her head rolled forward and then back. She was out of it.

At this moment I was so afraid. I thought about Emily. I remembered that I needed to be brave for Emily. I needed to get out of this for my daughter. I needed a plan.

My mind drifted to the terrifying probabilities. These men were probably going to kill me and Louise. I would never see Emily again. I felt suddenly sad and then I started to get angry.

I assessed the three men in the room. I certainly could not overpower them. Mr. Itchy Crotch reached for his nether regions. The man needed to see his doctor; maybe an anti-fungal cream? I smirked.

He caught me staring at him. "What are you laughing at?" he barked at me. Right then, I decided on my plan. If I could talk myself out of a job, then certainly I could talk myself out of this room. Or at least, I would attempt to until my last breath.

I crossed my arms across my chest, "Nothing. I'm not laughing at anything." I stared back at him. I wondered what their plan was. "So, now what happens, gentlemen?" The Brick Wall and Cat Video Guy looked a little uncomfortable.

"What do you think?" Mr. Itchy Crotch shot back. Okay, he was going to kill us. Got it! He was also in charge in this room.

"So, what are you waiting for?" I asked. The three exchanged glances again. They wanted to wait for their fourth partner; how nice. I looked down at my watch. That meant I had about four more hours to live. "So, are we waiting until five?" The Cat Video Guy shook his head. Mr. Itchy Crotch shook his finger at him. I smiled broadly.

"What are you smiling at?" he growled at me. I couldn't help but start laughing again—the Wicked Witch laugh. The three men looked horrified at me. Louise was looking at me now. Then her head lolled back again. I just shook my head. I was also aware of how badly I needed to pee.

"I'm sorry. I really have never done this before. It's just that I have so many questions. I'm also terrified," I spoke between cackles. "It would really help me stop if you'd answer my questions. I also have to pee like a racehorse." I let out an ear shattering peel of laughter.

"Okay, okay, just shut up," Mr. Itchy Crotch answered with disgust. Really? He thought I was disgusting because I had to pee? He was just lucky he didn't know what I called him in my head. I swallowed and lifted a hand. He quieted on my signal.

"Which one of you is in charge?" I once went on a date with a man who peppered me with questions. He asked question, after question, after question. I asked him if he listened to my answers. He said only sometimes. He was super annoying. I hoped that I would have the same repelling effect.

"We all are," Cat Video Guy announced proudly from behind the desk. Mr. Itchy Crotch looked like he wanted to say something, but held his tongue.

"Nah man, you know it's Mickey," the Brick Wall spoke. He sounded like a pillow was over his head. He really needed to get his nose checked. I could also smell the vomit on him.

"Mickey, Alicia's boyfriend?" I asked. Cat Video Guy didn't like my description. I wondered why.

"Yeah, that's right," the Brick Wall answered from the door.

"How is Alicia involved in this? Did Mickey drag her into this?" I shook my head in disgust. I knew what I was going to do. I would get them talking, maybe distracted.

"Alicia didn't know anything. She only helped a couple of times—just selling the stuff. She thought she was doing a favor. She ain't like that," Cat Video Guy clarified from behind his desk. He glared at me.

"She sold the stuff that you stole? Didn't she know it was stolen?" I pointed at the Brick Wall and he shook his head. "She thought she was doing a favor," he answered and smirked. Cat Video Guy folded his arms and pursed his lips. What was going on here? I leaned back in the chair.

"What about Ms. Butler's broach? Didn't she steal that?" The Brick Wall rolled his eyes.

"Nah, Mickey gave it to her. Told her not to wear it to work though." He shook his head as he asked, "Why are you asking all these questions?"

I shrugged my shoulders. I knew that I wanted to keep them talking for as long as possible. Maybe someone would come. Maybe I could figure a way out. I also wanted to know the truth. "I' curious and I love a good mystery," I answered him.

Mr. Itchy Crotch attempted to reach for his crotch, but I shot him a look. I shifted my attention to Cat Video Guy: "So, then, how did you get involved in this?"

"Alicia's my sister," he answered. Now I felt disgusted. He dragged his sister into this fiasco.

"Uh huh, so did Mickey have you delete the video or turn off the cameras?" He didn't respond. He looked ashamed. It started to come together for me. I sat up straighter in my chair. His eyes widened.

"Yeah?" I stared at him until he nodded his head. Louise made a little groan next to me while I calculated what I'd do next. I felt her forehead. She felt hot to me. I wasn't sure what that meant, but my worry grew.

I looked at the gun on the desk. He just left it there. I would need an opportunity, but right now I had to settle for some answers.

"So, you're Mr. Nelson?" Cat Video Guy gave me the side eye. At last it hit me. "Of course, your sister still uses her married name." He shook his head. So the woman at the antique store was Alicia, but she used her maiden name. "It was a smart move, using a nice woman like Alicia to sell the jewelry. No one would have pressed her about how she got it," I congratulated them, hoping to appeal to their egos.

Cat Video Guy leaned forward in his chair. "How did you know about that?" He was curious. All three sets of eyes were on me. They all appeared a little proud of themselves like they were the great criminal masterminds. I was filled with bravado. I might not be able to land any physical blows on these guys, but I knew that I could probably pummel them intellectually.

"Do you really want to know?" I whispered the question. The three men leaned in. I scooted my chair closer to the desk and I looked at each one.

"You're a detective, right?" Mr. Itchy Crotch guessed. He looked at the other three, sure in his guess.

"It's a little more complicated than that, boys," I answered. I hoped that I sounded enigmatic and calm. I could barely hold still because I needed to pee. The three looked back and forth. I thought I might lie to them and tell them that I was a police officer, but that could totally backfire.

I leaned closer to the desk. The gun was still too far to reach. I needed to find a way to get closer. Even if I could grab it, I still wouldn't know what to do, but I'd cross that bridge if I ever got to it.

"So, who are you?" Cat Video Guy asked. He was intrigued. I needed to keep them distracted as I moved closer to the gun.

"Who am I?" I repeated his question. I repeated the question again, this time I whispered it. I hoped I sounded a little frightening as I scrambled for some answers. I slid to the very edge of my chair.

"Are you a cop?" Cat Video Guy recoiled from the desk. I didn't want to say anything. I wasn't sure how they'd react. I decided to change the subject.

"Do you fellows mind if I move around? I really have to pee and I do better if I can move around." I broke the spell and the three leaned back and groaned, but I'd hooked them. They wanted to hear what I was going to say. "I'm serious. I really have to pee. You three are terrifying and are probably going to kill me. I think I have the right to say that I have to pee." I moved in the chair. I rocked it back and forth, shifting the chair a little forward with each shake. My chair was now next to the desk. The gun was equal distance between Cat Video Guy and me. I needed to get him further from the desk. I thought about my options. I could try to grab the gun now, but I needed better odds.

"How about getting me a glass of water? I'm not going anywhere," I addressed myself to Cat Video Guy. He scooted back in his chair and my opportunity appeared. I lunged for the gun. At the same time, Cat Video Guy lunged at his desk. My hand held the handle and his hand held the barrel. I yanked the gun straight up and the gun fired, shooting the ceiling, grazing his palm.

He cried out and let go of the gun. He held his hand close to him. I tried getting my other hand on the gun, but Mr. Itchy Crotch grabbed me around my shoulders, attempting to pull the weapon away. I twisted in his grip, stomping down on his foot and the gun went off again, this time striking the computer. I heard the Brick Wall behind me mutter a curse. Surely, someone heard the shots. Someone must be calling the police. I swung around again and the gun fired one more time. Lord, had that fool left his gun on his desk with the safety off?

I heard the Brick Wall's girly scream. The arms around me dropped as Mr. Itchy Crotch leaned over Brick Wall. The Brick Wall covered his face with his hand, like he might have been shot. A red and black welt rose up on the edge of his ear. The two looked at a bullet hole in the wall two inches from his shaved head.

They raised their hands in front of me. They looked terrified.

I held the firearm shakily. I saw Mr. Itchy Crotch shift his gaze behind me too late. Cat Video Guy grabbed me from behind and I dropped the gun on the floor. It fired again, striking the garbage can. Brick Wall screamed again. I kicked the gun under the desk. I flailed and kicked and at one point I'm pretty sure that I bit down on his arm. All I know is that my mouth filled with a lot of hair and there was definitely skin. He was going to need a tetanus shot.

In my flailing and kicking, my foot made direct contact with Mr. Itchy Crotch's crotch. He let out a gruff huff. He slid into the fetal position.

The door flew open, striking the Brick Wall. I heard him mutter "my nose." Standing in silhouette, holding a gun, was Jason. "Police, hands up!" he announced as he moved into the room. I heard Louise moan again from the corner. The three froze and I collapsed onto the floor with relief.

CHAPTER 34

"Ow! That hurts!" The nurse continued to examine my head. All around me I could hear buzzing and chirping from monitors. Touro Hospital's emergency room was busy this afternoon.

"Of course, it does; you have a goose egg the size of Kim Kardashian's butt back here." That was one image I didn't want associated with my head. She pressed a little more and I winced again. I heard her cluck her tongue. "I think that you'll be just fine, but the doctor will be in to give the all clear. I'll put some ice on that and your shoulder." She patted me gently on my other shoulder and stepped through a curtain and headed down a hallway.

I wondered what was happening with Louise. I knew that she was in one of these other beds, but I wasn't sure where. I thought briefly about exploring the area, but I was currently attached to a blood pressure cuff and some other monitor. The nurse returned with a broad smile on her face and two blue ice packs.

Doctor Martin followed her through the curtain. He immediately peppered the nurse about my condition. After his interrogation, he turned to me and smiled. I could see every capped tooth in his mouth.

"Denise, how are you?" He reached out and took my hand. The nurse placed the ice pack on my head and I sat up straighter. She placed the other on my shoulder.

"My head and my shoulder hurt, but I think that I'm okay." He wrinkled his forehand and pulled a pen light from the front pocket in his coat. He flashed the light in both my eyes.

"Looks like you don't have a concussion. I just want to tell you how brave we all think you were. What were you thinking taking on those men?" he asked in utter disbelief. I wasn't sure what I was thinking.

"Is Louise okay?" I wanted to know that she was all right and I wanted to get out of this place.

"She's sleepy and woozy. She'll have a hell of a hangover tomorrow, but she's going home in a little while. I wanted you to know that Riverview appreciates what you did, defending one of our residents. Why don't you take the rest of the week off? See you on Monday." With that, he turned around and walked through the curtain. "Also, say 'hello' to your mother for me," he said as he walked away.

I wanted to shake my head, but the ice pack would fall off. I held it in place, and I could feel it drip a little down my neck. Almost on Dr. Martin's heels, another doctor entered and checked me. He concurred with Dr. Martin's assessment. Then he left. I wondered how long it would take for them to release me.

As I sat there, in that noisy emergency room, I felt sad and relieved. Little by little, tears rolled down my cheeks. I thought about what might have happened in that security office. I thought about Tina Moore. I could feel my nose drip and I looked for a tissue. One was on the counter next to me, but just out of reach. I tried reaching for it when I saw a strong hand reach out and pluck out a few tissues. Jason handed me the tissues.

"Did you really break that guy's nose and throw up on him?" Jason asked the question with a smirk on his face. His chin on the left side looked red from the punch, but he still looked amazing. I could feel wet hair sticking to my forehead. I also realized that my sweater was torn at the shoulder, exposing my bra strap. I blushed.

"I might have done something like that. That sounds like me." I shook my head and the ice pack slipped and fell into my lap. We both laughed. Beautiful laugh lines deepened around his mouth. "So, you're a police officer?"

"Yes, I am," he answered proudly. He reached his right hand forward to shake my hand. "Officer Jason Stone." I shook his hand. He held onto my hand.

"You were investigating the thefts all along, am I right?" I wanted to know. He nodded his head. He stepped closer to the bed and smiled down at me.

"Yes, Dr. Martin approached us a few weeks ago and asked us to investigate the thefts. After his conversation with Tina Moore and other rumors, he suspected that some of the staff was involved. So, I went in." I felt a little silly now. I wondered if I had just been in the way the whole time.

"Did I help?" I asked quietly. His smile widened. Wow, he was one good-looking man.

"You did. We couldn't connect them all until you and Ms. Butler went to Ms. Cramer about Alicia." He touched my cheek. "You also scared the hell out of those guys. They won't shut up. I think they thought we were partners, and I was the good cop." He laughed at the image, but I kind of liked the fantasy of being his partner. I also liked the idea of those three goons thinking that I was the bad cop.

His expression became somber. "You kind of scared me." I squeezed his hand. I felt frightened too.

"What about Ms. Cramer?" I asked, drawing in a shaky breath. I wanted to push the afternoon's episode from my mind before I burst into tears.

"She actually called the police and spoke with our detectives about what had happened with Tina Moore.

While she didn't cause Ms. Moore's death, she did leave her to die. She will have something to answer for. I don't know how you convinced Ms. Cramer to go to the police, but it really helped. You also brought a great deal of peace to Tina Moore's mother." I smiled at him. "You have good instincts."

"Thanks." I also have nice legs, but he didn't mention that. He pushed my hair behind my ear and leaned forward. I figured this was it. He was going to kiss me. Finally, the ultimate pay off for risking my behind for an old woman and uncovering the mystery of a young woman's death. This was it.

I closed my eyes and felt his lips touch my forehead. The gesture was so tender and sweet. I was so disappointed, but at least I got kissed, I guess. My eyes fluttered open and I heard the squeal of little girl—my little girl. Jason stepped back and released my hand.

"Mommy, mommy! I love you!" Emily shouted. She let go of my mother's hand and raced toward the hospital bed.

Emily climbed into the bed with me and my mother stood on the opposite side of the bed from Jason. She wrapped her arms around my neck and planted a wet kiss on my cheek. The monitor next to the bed chirped loudly. She held onto my neck for dear life. I held onto her. I felt my earlier disappointment evaporate.

"I'll give you a call sometime." Jason nodded and left. I waved at him as he walked away. I squeezed Emily. I hoped I'd see him again.

CHAPTER 35

Over the next few days, my head and shoulder healed quickly. The bruises on my shoulder faded to yellow. I spoke with the police at the station. I relished telling how I'd solved a mystery, an actual mystery. The officers graciously allowed me to revel in my success, even if they were already on the case. While I was at the station, I only saw a glimpse of Jason as I gave my statement. I also saw Officer Perez who congratulated me on helping the police break open their case. I felt good. By Saturday, I felt fully recovered from my injuries. That evening, I decided to go out with Carrie for a drink at St. Joe's Bar on Magazine Street. I also texted Jason and invited him to come by and see us.

Carrie and I laughed, seated on red benches on the patio in the back of the bar. I told her what had happened. She just shook her head. "This is why I need your help on my screenplay." In the corner of my eye, I thought that I caught a glimpse of Jason. A bald man stood at the bar in the other room. When he pivoted, I realized it wasn't Jason. The bald man winked at me.

Later that evening, while lying in bed, I heard my phone ding. I checked my phone. I'd received a text from Jason: "Sorry I missed you tonight. I'll see you soon." I held the phone to my chest.

On Monday morning, I contemplated calling in sick at Riverview. I flopped back and forth in the bed, willing myself back asleep. I wondered if I should go ahead and quit, but then again, I still needed a job. It might not be much revenue, but it was something.

I dropped Emily off and headed to work. I rolled down Broadway Avenue toward the levy. I could hear a rumbling of thunder. I guess this meant the end of the lovely October weather.

When I arrived, the receptionist stopped me at the front desk. The woman directed me to sit at one of the benches in the lobby until the administrator was available. I wondered what this was about. I suspected they might want to dismiss me.

After what felt like an eternity, a young woman wearing glasses and a grey pinstriped suit approached me. She held a large manila folder in front of her. "Ms. Reed, would you follow me?"

I followed her around the receptionist's desk and into Ms. Cramer's office. The desk was stacked high with files. She directed me to one of the folding chairs and I sat as she moved around the desk. She put her file on one of the stacks and tsked under her breath.

"Ms. Reed, I'm Deidra Clark, the interim administrator. Dr. Martin directed me to debrief you after the events of last week. How are you?" I nodded my head and was about to speak when she went on, "Good, you look good, and the hospital said that you would make a full recovery from your injuries." She looked down and read a file on her desk. "We just want to make sure that you're completely happy here at Riverview."

She looked at me expectantly. I knew this trick. This was how you got someone to quit. I was not falling for this one again.

"I think that other than being threatened, breaking open a theft case, answering some questions about the death of a former Riverview employee and bonking my head on a bad guy's nose, that my time at Riverview has been quite lovely," I answered. She pushed back her glasses and raised an eyebrow at me. I leaned back in my chair and raised an eyebrow at Ms. Clark.

"So, you aren't thinking about quitting?" she asked. She leaned forward on her desk and knocked a few files off her desk. She slumped in her chair and reached to the floor for the files.

"I am not thinking about quitting. Are you?" I asked innocently. Ms. Clark sat straight up in her seat and pushed back her glasses.

"Heavens, no! I'm happy here. Really happy, I love it!" she answered with an air of paranoia. She looked around like she was looking for secret cameras. She composed herself. "Why would you ask me that?" She leaned forward. "What did you hear? You can't tell something, can you?"

"I beg your pardon?"

"Nothing." She looked back at her file. She cleared her throat. "So, you want to continue at Riverview?" She looked up at me.

"Yes, I suppose."

She nodded her head. I nodded my head and smiled.

"That's wonderful. We want you to continue at Riverview, of course. We just have some forms here that we need to fill out. A waiver and an acknowledgment that Riverview had nothing to do with those thefts and your injuries and that you won't hold us responsible." She held a paper out to me. I took it from her and read the tiny print. At the bottom, there was a place for my signature. I signed the sheet and she blew out her breath.

"I'm so glad that you signed that. Also, due to budget constraints and the restructuring of this administrative position and the security department and so on, it's just that—we've had to reduce your hours." She spoke the last part as quickly as possible into her file folder and looked over the top of her glasses at me. She frowned.

"So, I'm part, part time?" She nodded her head and lifted the file like it was a shield. I folded my arms across my chest. Great. I was not unemployed. I was now officially underemployed. She mouthed, "Sorry."

I left her office and checked with the receptionist for my new schedule. I rolled my eyes at the paper. I wasn't even supposed to come in today. I wandered to the elevators and pushed the button.

I made my way to Louise's apartment and knocked on her door. She swung the door open and immediately threw her arms around me. She smiled at me as she held me.

"Denise, I'm so happy to see you! Please come in." She invited me to take a seat in my usual spot. She took her place across from me. Both our gazes fell to the red stain on her carpet.

"I'm a little foggy on what happened last week, Denise, but I know that you saved my life." She spoke earnestly. "The last thing I remember clearly is hanging up the phone and then offering the boys some sherry before bed. One of those dolts hit me. He made me spill my sherry. Then the other grabbed my arm, but I don't remember anything else. They must have drugged me."

I nodded my head. "They did." She leaned back in her chair and shivered. She rubbed her hands together, as if trying to warm herself.

"And Ms. Cramer? She was involved in Tina's death? She was the reason Tina was in the street? She didn't help Tina while she was dying?" Louise was disgusted. I just nodded. "Was she part of the thefts?"

"No, but she found out that the two guards weren't recording or monitoring the video system. She thought it was incompetence. Heck, I thought they were just incompetent too. It took me a little while to realize that they were involved. Turns out that Lawrence Nelson and Alicia Jones are brother and sister. She got her brother to shut off the cameras when her boyfriend Mickey and Brick Wall went into the residents' rooms to steal. Then she'd sell the items," I said. Louise raised an eyebrow. "Let me start from the beginning, Louise."

I began the story, starting with my cereal fueled suspicion about Ms. Cramer after reading the article about Tina Moore. I filled her in on my interaction with Melinda and then my discovery of Louise's disappearance. Finally, I told her about my brave and glorious battle in the security room, followed by Jason's arrival. We both laughed.

"Did you really throw up on him?" Everyone seemed to focus on that one part. Louise delighted in that detail.

"I also fell on top of him, broke his nose, filled the air with creepy hysterical laughter, and dropped a firearm repeatedly." I puffed out my chest and then mimed barfing. Louise howled with laughter. She wiped a tear from the corner of her eye, and composed herself.

"I guess we won't see each other as much, now that you saved the day. You'll probably need to find another job," Louise said sadly. She stood up and walked to her window.

"Maybe not as much, but you'll still see me." I would need to keep looking for another full time position, but something told me that we would see a lot of each other. I was determined that I would see her. "Louise, you're my friend. I will see you." She turned around and smiled at me.

"Good." She walked to her kitchen and returned with the sherry. "Let's drink to that!"

The End

ABOUT THE AUTHOR

 Mary E. Koppel is a New Orleans' girl living right off Route 66! A mother, traveler and lover of mystery and romance, Mary is blessed with constant curiosity that has only gotten her into a little bit of trouble. She has written one book of essays, co-authored a book of non-fiction, and she has written essays and devotions for a few blogs and publications. This is Mary's first novel.